RAGE UNDER
THE ARCTIC

By Basil Jackson

Epicenter
Rage Under the Arctic

The North Star's Course

BASIL JACKSON

RAGE UNDER THE ARCTIC

W · W · NORTON & COMPANY · INC ·

NEW YORK

FIRST EDITION
Library of Congress Cataloging in Publication Data
Jackson, Basil, 1920–
  Rage under the Arctic.
  I. Title.
PZ4.J127Rag3   [PR9199.J3]   813'.5'4   73–8991
ISBN 0–393–08379–9
Published simultaneously in Canada
by George J. McLeod Limited, Toronto
PRINTED IN THE UNITED STATES OF AMERICA

1 2 3 4 5 6 7 8 9 0

ACKNOWLEDGMENTS

I wish to thank Benjamin F. Ackerman, former lieutenant commander, Royal Canadian Navy, officer responsible for submarine rescue, a diver and Arctic specialist; Dr. P. D. McTaggart-Cowan, executive director, Science Council of Canada and head of the Task Force responsible for the *Arrow* oil spill clean-up; and Ronald M. Wineberg, electronics engineer, Litton Systems (Canada) Ltd., for their help with certain of the technical information in this book.

AUTHOR'S NOTE

U.S. Coast Guard officers in San Francisco Bay stood by help-lessly one January night in 1971 as two dots on the radar screen merged. They could not prevent two Standard Oil Company of California oil tankers from colliding and spilling eight hundred and forty thousand gallons of Bunker C oil into the bay. TWO OIL TANKERS COLLIDE—GIANT BAY OIL SLICK, ran the headline next morning. More than sixty miles of beaches were fouled by gooey oil, and seven thousand seabirds were killed.

In 1967 the tanker *Torrey Canyon* crashed into a charted reef off the English coast. It was a clear day. All her radar systems were operating perfectly. Twenty-two million gallons of oil spewed into the sea. Beaches and rocks for hundreds of miles along the English and French coasts were blackened. Headlines blazed across the front pages of the world's newspapers; television cameras whirled.

The Liberian tanker *Arrow*, under charter to Imperial Oil Limited, piled on a rock in Chedabucto Bay, Nova Scotia, in February 1970, and two and a half million gallons of Bunker C oil poured into the sea. For the first time clean-up experts had to contend with oil on ice-covered waters and frozen beaches. Again, there was widespread newspaper, television and radio coverage.

9

AUTHOR'S NOTE

In United States waters alone more than seven thousand oil spills occur each year. Few make the headlines. Before the collision in San Francisco Bay there had been one hundred and ten disastrous oil and chemical spills in 1968, one hundred and eighty six in 1969, and two hundred and thirteen in 1970. The U.S. Coast Guard reports a 500 percent increase in *reported* oil spills in the past five years.

More than one and a quarter *billion* gallons (five million tons) of petroleum products, including crude oil, are spilled directly into the world's oceans every year, according to the Environmental Protection Agency in Washington, D. C. Oil dumped into rivers pours another ten million tons into the oceans. For example, consider the car you drive. Some of its oil ends up in the street sewers and ultimately enters the sea. An estimated two hundred and forty thousand gallons of oil from cars and industrial machinery flow through the sewers of Schenectady, New York, every year, and the volume is increasing.

Calculated on a nationwide basis, six billion gallons of waste automobile oil enters all the sewer systems of the United States every year and flows into the sea.

Underwater explorer Jacques-Yves Cousteau says that if pollution of the seas doesn't stop, then "Maybe thirty, forty or fifty years will see the end of everything."

Thor Heyerdahl, testifying on the destruction of the oceans before a United States Senate subcommittee, said that he encountered globs of oil for forty-three of the fifty-seven days he spent drifting across the Atlantic on the raft *Ra*.

At least three countries, the United States, Britain and Japan, have on their drawing boards designs for large commercial submarines to be used to carry cargo—including oil—under the ice of the Arctic seas.

One U.S. proposal is for a nuclear-powered submarine tanker to ferry oil under the ice of the Northwest Passage, where the vessel will be protected from surface storms and heavy seas, from Prudhoe Bay, Alaska, to East Coast ports. The Arctic Institute of America, conservationists, and ecologists are alarmed about the

AUTHOR'S NOTE

prospect of a major oil spill in the Arctic seas. They are not convinced about safety, even by an opinion such as the one voiced by Commander William R. Anderson, U.S.N., captain of the U.S.S. *Nautilus*, the first submarine to journey under the ice to the North Pole, on August 3, 1958: "Across the top of the world, blazed by thousands of instrument readings, lies a maritime highway of tomorrow—strategic, commercially promising, and, I am convinced, safe." (*National Geographic*, January 1959.)

The Arctic ice pack controls the temperature of a large area of the Northern Hemisphere, including the United States, Canada, and Europe. A major oil spill in the Arctic could have dire consequences for the atmospheric environment of these regions, for the northern seas comprise the only unpolluted reservoir of water on earth; the water that flows south in a massive circulatory movement to cleanse and replenish the seas in the Temperate Zone.

John Volpe, former United States Secretary of Transportation, says: "We are determined that effective controls and procedures be established to prevent pollution of the Arctic waters and ice fields which could damage the environment of the area and possibly that of the entire earth."

The chilling conclusion of the United States President's Panel on Oil Spills: "The United States does not have at this time sufficient technical or operational ability to cope satisfactorily with a large-scale oil spill in the marine environment."

In my story, the submarine tanker *North Star* is a product of my imagination, as is the company that owns and operates her, Prudhoe-Northwest Passage Corporation. But the growing danger to the ice-covered northern seas is not imagined. The threat is real: the danger is more critical than in warmer waters because of the finely balanced ecology of the Arctic. These once lonely waters are now threatened by risk of tanker collision, by oil discharged from the bilge tanks of an increasing number of supply ships and seismic survey vessels operating in the Arctic along with naval ships and submarines, and by the risk of leaks from offshore and land-based oil-drilling rigs. These are sprouting like mushrooms in the far north, as scientists seek new sources of oil for the estimated doubling of the world's oil consumption needs in the next decade and as the energy crisis becomes more acute.

As far back as 1954 an International Conference for Prevention of the Pollution of the Sea by Oil was held. After much argument broad limits on oil pollution were agreed on, but ships were still allowed to discharge oil at sea. Another conference was held in 1969 to tighten controls. Of the forty-nine nations attending, twenty-nine countries—including Panama, Honduras, Liberia, Greece, and Japan, whose flags fly from hundreds of oil tankers —refused to sign for tighter controls.

Attempts by the United Nations to get the maritime nations to agree to tough, internationally administered antipollution laws have failed. It will be too late to enforce realistic regulations after a catastrophe occurs.

During the research for this book, checking into the methods used, interviewing oil clean-up experts and Arctic undersea explorers, I was struck by the lack of effective means to fight oil spills. No method of solidifying oil on water so that it can be towed away in chunks has yet been developed; we are forced to work with imperfect techniques. The official report of the *Arrow* clean-up, *Task Force, Operation Oil*, bluntly puts it on the line: "The *Arrow* disaster revealed dramatically and at substantial cost the woefully inadequate measures in being for contending with oil spills of this magnitude."

Concerned people all over the world agonize over the coming danger. The catastrophe may not occur in the way I have described it, but the law of probability ensures that it will occur. The question today is not *how?* but *when?*

Basil Jackson

RAGE UNDER
THE ARCTIC

ONE

For five days he had not been able to use the periscope. That was a long time to run at top speed on instruments alone—especially for a man whose submarine training and experience went back to World War II.

Now, as he peered into the scope, it took a moment for Millwood's eyes to adjust from the brilliance of his control room to the flat, gray light outside. Gradually the midnight sun came into focus, suspended low over a calm sea dotted with small ice cakes. Far off to the north the aurora flickered against a darker sky.

He was aware of the four others behind him, waiting. An odd quartet, he thought, but reliable, the very best, an experienced crew with the highest technical qualifications. A level-headed first officer, a first-class female electronics engineer, a trusty nuclear power engineer, and an oil tycoon passenger. Times had changed.

"The sea's almost clear," he said, turning to his second-in-command. "Take a look, Harding. Prudhoe Bay is just over the horizon. Or maybe it should be ladies first," he laughed, turning to Eva Zachrisson. She grasped the periscope handle and bent over the glass, her straight hair falling around it. "It's beautiful!" she exclaimed. "So peaceful. And look— the aurora borealis! What magnificent colors!" She looked up at Millwood, and he saw the excitement in her eyes.

Harding took his turn at the periscope and Simoncelli moved in behind him. "Let me have a look," Simoncelli said. Moving his huge bulk in front of Millwood, he elbowed Harding away from the periscope.

"Jesus Christ! Isn't that a sight! Just like the old days on the oil fields—with the midnight sun and the northern lights."

Crane, the taciturn middle-aged power engineer, took his turn at the scope, grunted, and disappeared aft, presumably to check his engines again.

"How long did you say it'll take to get the crude aboard, Frank?" Simoncelli asked.

"About ten hours," Millwood said. "Sixty million gallons is a big load."

"I can't wait to see it on its way to New Jersey." Simoncelli pulled a cigar from the breast pocket of his corduroy jacket and stuck it in his mouth at a jaunty angle.

Millwood was pleased to see Simoncelli's exuberance. His oil-magnate passenger had a big stake on the success of this voyage. The way he had persuaded the oil companies owning Prudhoe Bay oil leases to finance the project had hit *Wall Street Journal* headlines for weeks, and he understood Simoncelli had a hell of a lot of his personal fortune tied up in the venture when he'd been the central figure in setting up the Prudhoe-Northwest Passage Corporation for the purpose of designing, building and operating the world's first commercial tanker submarine. Whether the company went ahead with *North Star*'s sister subs—a total of twenty had been projected —depended on the success of their return trip to the East Coast loaded to the gunwales with Prudhoe crude.

Millwood felt a sense of relief now that *North Star* was running just below the surface of a sea almost clear of ice. The days below the solid pack ice of the Northwest Passage, with the navigation of the vessel entirely in the hands of the computerized navigation system and the programmed sonar buoys spaced under the polar seas, had been wearing on his nerves. Instinctively, he'd wanted everything to be under the direct control of his brain, his muscles, his senses. All his training, experience, and habits were against the total surrender to Eva's precious "Auto Nav." He had to force himself to adjust. But then, there were a lot of other differences between this huge tanker sub and his old Navy boats: the ability to carry sixty million gallons of crude oil; an underwater speed of thirty knots; the electronics, external television viewers for under-ice navigation, and the upward, downward, and forward-facing anticollision sonars that kept the vessel automatically at a safe distance below the ice to avoid collision with underwater obstructions like the bottom of icebergs.

The complex systems had brought them safely, "hands off," all the way from Boston to Alaska. They had worked so efficiently, *North Star* might almost have made the trip without a crew.

He turned to Eva. "Switch off the Auto Nav. We'll go up on manual. Harding, stand by to open the forward hatch when we surface." He pressed a button, and the periscope whined down into the control room. Eva bent over her electronics console and pressed a button. A red light on the console changed to green. "Auto Nav disengaged, Captain," she announced. Millwood, sitting in a high leather chair, grasped a lever and pulled it back. It was a relief as last to take over control of his submarine manually. Operating the diving and surfacing lever was something he normally would order his second-in-command to do; but there was so little to do on this submarine that he grasped at every opportunity for action now that they were under manual control. As the lever clicked home, he felt the seat slant sharply upward.

"Hey!" exclaimed Simoncelli, grabbing the periscope housing.

Millwood glanced in his direction to make sure he was secure. As he moved the lever forward, the floor leveled. The remote sound of waves slapping on the hull signaled that *North Star* had surfaced.

Millwood was the first to move. As he climbed the ladder into the steel conning tower—called the "sail" now—where the bridge was located, he heard Harding following and stood aside as his second punched a button. Instantly a hatch slid open on silent rails, revealing a square of sky and blue sea. The interior of the sail was flooded with cold, clear air.

"It smells sweet," Millwood heard Eva say at the base of the ladder. "Everybody out!" he called, and stepped onto the small platform built around the sail. Harding followed, then Eva. Millwood waited for Simoncelli to lumber up the ladder and squeeze his body through the hatch before he walked around the platform. Crane poked his head out and grunted with satisfaction. Millwood sucked a deep draft of air into his lungs and released it in a long sigh. *North Star*'s oxygen-making equipment and complex air-conditioning system had provided air during the long days and nights below the ice, but there was nothing like the real thing.

He took another lungful and scanned the horizon. Due south the sky merged into a gray line where it met the sea. The midnight sun cast a dim but surprisingly clear light across the water, and overhead the aurora flickered in long streaks of gold. It was a scene of calm isolation. Even Simoncelli was silenced by its beauty.

"Hand me the sextant, Harding," Millwood said. He brought the instrument, and Millwood adjusted the vernier knobs and focused on the pale northern sun. A few minutes later, after rapid calculations, he looked up. "Right on the button!" he said. "Latitude and longitude correspond exactly with the Auto Nav readout. Radio Prudhoe. Give our position and estimated time of arrival, and contact Boston." He glanced at his watch. "It'll be nine in the morning there. Herbert Armstrong should be in by now."

Millwood followed Harding down the ladder, leaving the other three on the platform. They all needed a change of scene, he reflected; Simoncelli more than Eva and Crane, who were used to shipboard life. He felt a deep sense of personal responsibility for his elderly passenger's welfare. Simoncelli, he knew, was not in the best of health, despite his size and years of outdoor living, and he wanted the old warrior to get pleasure from this maiden voyage; especially from seeing the crude oil he had invested in being shipped east.

Harding picked up the radio telephone, turned the knob on the radio console to the correct wave band, and handed Millwood the phone.

"Submarine tanker *North Star* calling Prudhoe Bay," he said. "Over."

"Hello, *North Star!*" The reply was so instantaneous that Millwood jerked the phone away from his ear. He stepped forward and flicked a switch on the panel. The concealed overhead speakers burst with the exuberance of the voice from the oil field. "We've got everything ready for a big celebration. Congratulations!"

"You've got Prudhoe!" shouted Simoncelli, who had climbed laboriously down the ladder behind Eva, and now stood in the control room.

"Here's Mr. Blake, the boss," the voice announced. After

a brief crackle of static a placid voice said, "Hello, *North Star*." Although the voice was calm Millwood detected an undertone of excitement. "Welcome to Prudhoe Bay, Captain Millwood and crew! Did you have a good voyage? What is your position?"

"Captain Millwood speaking. Everything went fine. We surfaced ten minutes ago and are proceeding due south at twenty-five knots." He read off the vessel's position, adding: "That's about one hundred miles due north of you. We should be alongside in two hours fifty minutes. Please stand by while we radio Boston."

"Okay, Captain. Standing by."

Harding switched to the company wave band and the room filled with a howl of static through which they could hear a series of cracks like the snapping of sticks. Eva put both hands over her ears. The speakers screeched as Harding disengaged the tuning control and rotated a knob. "It's no use," he said, switching off.

"Let me try," Eva said, brushing Harding aside. She pressed a series of buttons but the speakers continued to shriek. After a few moments she gave up and said, "I'm sorry, Captain. Shall I call Prudhoe back?"

He nodded. As she switched wave bands he observed a slight slump of her shoulders. He took over the instrument.

"Prudhoe, this is Captain Millwood of submarine *North Star*. Due to heavy interference we can't get through to Boston. Please signal Herbert Armstrong, president, Prudhoe-Northwest Passage Corporation, Boston. Tell him Captain Frank Millwood sends his compliments and reports that submarine *North Star* surfaced approximately one hundred miles due north of Prudhoe Bay after an uneventful voyage and is expected to tie up at the company's Prudhoe terminal at approximately noon Eastern Standard time. We're proceeding on manual control. Everybody on board is well and——"

"Tell him to get ready to kiss the golden barrel!" Simoncelli shouted.

"Oscar Simoncelli says, get ready for the symbolic golden barrel of oil. End of message. Over."

"Message received, Captain. I'll relay it immediately. We're looking forward to seeing you all, sir. So long for now."

Millwood accepted the rum and Coke but turned down the caviar. "I don't like it," he bluntly told one of the oil field roughnecks who had been pressed into service as a waiter in the lofty wooden mess hall. There were more than two hundred men sitting around the long tables. Blake, in charge of the company's Prudhoe Bay operations, sat at his right, a colorful figure in a red checkered shirt. Simoncelli sat on his left, near Crane, next to Eva, and Millwood was aware of the effect she had on the oil drillers. An attractive young woman was obviously a rarity on the base; the only other females Millwood could see were two elderly Eskimoes working in the kitchen. Harding sat farther down the table, laughing as he drank and talked with the oilman next to him.

Blake, a well-built man of about fifty-five, suddenly rose and banged the table with a spoon. "Gentlemen, gentlemen," he shouted, "and lady!" He beamed at Eva amid cheers and wolf whistles. "It gives me great pleasure to call on Captain Millwood to cut the cake." He picked up a knife and turned toward Millwood. "All yours, Captain!"

The kitchen door swung open and, accompanied by loud cheers, two oilmen carried in a huge, unevenly iced cake and placed it in front of Millwood. When the din subsided Millwood rose to read aloud the inscription. "Welcome *North*

Star. Good luck on your voyage east." Turning to Blake, he proclaimed: "On behalf of my crew, and passenger, thank you all very much." He sliced the cake and sat down, relieved that the formalities, such as they were, were over. As the party started to break up he turned to Blake. "When will you be ready to pump the crude aboard?"

Blake looked at his watch. "They must be almost ready now. Let's check it out."

The station wagon drew up on the edge of the gravel road. Millwood tamped the ground with his boot as he got out. "I hear you have to be extra careful how you treat the ground up here," he said. "What effect does the gravel have on the permafrost?"

"The oil company has a strict policy about the environment," Blake said, sounding well rehearsed and prepared to deliver a lecture. Millwood knew of the guided tours of the mammoth oil depot the corporation had arranged for worried ecologists. "The permafrost goes down two thousand feet in these parts. We've been extra careful. The gravel here"—he pointed with a gnarled finger—"is about six feet thick. It acts as an insulator and prevents the underlying permafrost from melting. Make a hell of a mess if it thawed!"

"There's a lot of rock in the permafrost itself, besides the gravel," Harding put in.

"Harding, here, is our expert on rocks," Millwood explained. "He's a rockhound. Where does the gravel come from?"

"We ship it in from the alluvial flats near the rivers around Prudhoe. We take it out carefully so's not to disturb the spawning grounds of the fish." He looked across the level landscape studded with blue lagoons amid the rough tundra grass and walked on, guiding them between the rows of orange-painted wooden buildings, explaining as he went. "Here's where the men sleep and have their recreational facilities. The mess hall where we've just been is where we usually eat. It's open twenty-four hours a day because we work round the clock, in shifts."

Millwood pointed to the foundation of a building they were passing. "Why are the buildings raised off the ground on stilts like that?"

"To prevent the heat in them from melting the permafrost. If it melted, they'd tip over," Blake replied succinctly. Millwood got the feeling Blake had explained this all many times before.

"Is that why the pipeliners are thinking of putting their pipes on stilts?"

"Yes. But they're laying them in beds of gravel now. The caribou herds wouldn't pass under the raised pipes."

"Are there caribou here?" Eva asked excitedly.

"There are two herds on the North Slope during the summer. They're due in camp about now," Blake replied. "There's a herd east of here, in the National Wildlife Range. And another farther west, near the Colville River. They come through in season and stroll around the rigs. They're used to us now. They'd be all right if the do-gooder conservationists would leave them alone," he added with conviction.

"How do you mean?" Millwood asked.

"These conservationist fellas stir up trouble. They get the public aroused over something we can handle ourselves. As long as we take all the necessary precautions the Arctic ecology won't be affected: like the safeguards for preventing oil spills. If you want my opinion, it's more dangerous to ship sixty million gallons of crude oil under the ice, in spite of your safety systems."

Millwood wondered what a landlubber like Blake could

possibly know about the safety systems aboard *North Star*.

"You said the conservationists should leave the caribou alone," he persisted. "What do you mean, do they disturb them?"

"Well, they don't exactly disturb them," Blake said guardedly. "It's the bad publicity they make for all the oil companies, and the same with the oil spills. They act as though we're only out to make a profit and to hell with the environment!"

"The Arctic ecology is more delicately balanced than any other," said Millwood. "I heard of a bulldozer operator who scraped the initials of his oil company two hundred feet long in the tundra and the sun thawed the permafrost. Ten years later the surface scrapes had eroded to ditches eight feet deep. I've heard that if you just *walk* across the tundra you disturb the thin layer of subsoil and thereby destroy the tiny ecosystem of wild flowers, spiders, and miniature trees."

Blake eyed Millwood with a mixture of surprise and suspicion, but Millwood ignored him and turned toward the terminal where *North Star* lay at her mooring. He was impatient to begin loading the oil cargo. His movement attracted the others' attention to the gray-blue shape that rode quietly alongside the massive steel structure supported on piling deeply driven into the permafrost. For the hundredth time since he'd seen *North Star* take shape in the shipyard, he ran his eye over her thousand-foot length. Her slender sail, as tall as a two-story building, loomed high over the terminal. She had a blunt, shark-nosed bow and flattened sides, which he knew the shipyard architects had cunningly designed for absolute maximum oil storage. Once *North Star* was loaded, he and his companions would be almost entirely surrounded by oil—working, sleeping, and eating in a womb surrounded by the amniotic fluid of their cargo.

A man in grubby, oil-stained overalls approached Blake.

"Everything's ready, sir," he reported. "The connections have been checked and the on-loading pumps are at stand-by."

"Okay, Jim." Blake turned to Millwood. "You'll want to show us where the connections are on *North Star*, Captain."

"Then let's go aboard. There are two forward and four aft."

He looked at the distant silver tanks beyond the oil rigs, and his eyes traced the thick pipes leading away on steel trestles supported on the familiar stilts. "How long has the oil been out of the ground?" he demanded.

"About a month," replied Blake, with the air of a man who'd done his homework thoroughly. Millwood again got the impression that Blake had expected the question. "It's cold," Blake added. Millwood grunted. He thought of the hull distortion that would take place if they pumped in oil fresh out of the ground, at 180 degrees Fahrenheit. The hot oil, plus its pressure inside the hull, would damage *North Star* irreparably: the welded joints would buckle and leak, the seals on the on-board booster pumps disintegrate, and the complex pipework warp. Even with her double outside skin, the submarine's hull would be dangerously strained and the structural integrity of their control room threatened. The damage a careless oilman could do by screwing the wrong coupling to the submarine's tank connections would be so extensive that Millwood shuddered at the thought.

As the sun dipped to its lowest point, Millwood walked down the gangplank. The loading had gone off without a hitch, and the submarine, he observed with satisfaction, was riding high in the water. The massive oil cargo now replaced the water ballast they had carried on the outward voyage. Although it was the first time that *North Star* had been filled with her designated load, Millwood knew from the vessel's sea tests, when he had simulated cargo and ballast loads using water, that she could be trimmed to neutral buoyancy when he put to sea and partially filled the ballast tanks with water.

"What do your cargo gauges register?" he asked Blake, standing with the oil crew foreman at the pumping station on the terminal. The foreman produced a scrap of oil-stained paper on which he had scribbled some figures. "Sixty million, one hundred and five thousand gallons, sir," he replied. "A bonus," he added, laughing. Millwood compared the figures with those he had written into the logbook and remarked, "You're short one barrel."

Blake gave Millwood an anxious look. The foreman appeared puzzled. "The golden barrel!" Millwood laughed.

Blake and the foreman looked relieved. "I was planning that for the morning. Before you sailed, Captain," he said seriously. "The light'll be better for photographs. In the meantime you and your crew are to be our guests. I've arranged sleeping quarters in House One. It's not exactly the Ritz-Carlton but everything's comfortable and——"

"What about security for *North Star?*" Millwood cut him short. "Have you got guards?"

"Uh, no," Blake said. Millwood marveled at a mentality that gave no thought to proper security arrangements. "Then we'll sleep aboard," he snapped.

"We could set up a guard," Blake said feebly. "We've never had need for a security force. Not with working around the clock."

Millwood looked at the open water sparkling beyond *North Star*'s mooring lines. Some crude oil had dripped overboard when the loading pipelines had been uncoupled. The splotch of oil grew in an expanding arc of color. He shuddered and looked away. This wasn't the Navy, he reminded himself. Perhaps he'd been too harsh. "All right," he said at last. "You pick a guard from your men, and I'll put Mr. Harding in charge to arrange their shifts. Mr. Harding will stay aboard all night and Mr. Simoncelli, Mrs. Zachrisson, Mr. Crane, and I will be pleased to accept your hospitality."

"That's fine, Captain. I'll get my men organized," said Blake, and hurried away.

Millwood slept poorly. Once he got up and pulled back the heavy drapes. The midnight sun lit the base, casting the tall oil rigs in the distance into sharp relief. By standing at the side of the window and pressing close to the double pane he could see *North Star*'s bow, a brilliant blue where the highlights bounced from the reflection in the still waters. He yawned and looked at his watch. Three thirty; hell of a time to be awake. He hadn't had an unbroken night's sleep since Betty died, he ruminated gloomily. Not since he'd received that awesome radio signal at sea two years ago, the flat unfeeling voice announcing she'd been killed in an auto accident.

He let the drape fall, stretched his arms wide, and flung himself on the bed. With a bit of luck he might still catch another couple of hours of sleep before sailing time.

TWO

Millwood looked up as the golden barrel swung overhead. The crane operator on the terminal carefully lowered it to the foredeck, and a couple of husky oilmen heaved it through the hatch to a roar of cheers from their mates lining the terminal rail. Before it was lowered into the control room, where it would be secured, Millwood yanked off the filler cap and shone a flashlight into the barrel's interior.

"Just to be sure nobody put oil in it by mistake," he explained, smiling. With Simoncelli chain-smoking cigars he couldn't take risks. "Okay, lower away."

As they took it down the ladder it occurred to him with satisfaction that he was reversing the procedure that the mammoth S.S. *Manhattan* tanker-icebreaker had followed on her historic voyage through the Northwest Passage to Prudhoe in 1969. The *Manhattan* had carried a solitary barrel filled with crude back to the East Coast, but her cargo tanks had been completely empty; hers had been a proving voyage only. And here he was with filled-to-the-brim cargo tanks and an empty golden barrel, an old oil drum that Blake had painted gold. "See that it's lashed down securely!" he called below to Harding.

Blake hurried up the gangplank, shouting, "Good luck, Captain! Safe trip home!" He shook Millwood's hand and then Simoncelli's. "Any final instructions?"

"Get your radio operator to signal Boston as soon as you go ashore. Give them our time of sailing. That's all."

"And keep pumping up that black gold!" Simoncelli cried, slapping Blake on the back. "*North Star* will be back for more. And, pretty soon, her sister subs!"

Blake took Eva's hand. "I hope you'll come back, Mrs. Zachrisson," he said. "We get hungry for the sight of good-looking women up here!"

Millwood nodded for Eva and Simoncelli to go through the hatch. Crane was already aboard. When the two oilmen had gone ashore, Harding took up a position near the mooring lines.

"Cast off forward!" Millwood called. Harding relayed the instructions and the ropes swung free.

"Cast off aft!"

Millwood stood behind the bridge lookout and surveyed the control panel. He put a hand on a lever and simultaneously pressed a button. A faint tremor strummed through his feet as the engines came to life. He moved the lever forward and grasped the wheel on the panel, and the distance between the terminal and the submarine widened as *North Star* gathered speed. The vessel slid effortlessly between the lines of buoys that marked the passage dredged from the shallows in the bay. In twenty minutes the terminal was an oblong the size of a domino tile and the oil rigs were matchsticks behind the distant silver storage tanks.

Millwood looked at the sky. A good weather forecast had come over the Prudhoe teleprinter from the airport at Anchorage. Solid polar ice was at least two hundred miles farther north at this time of year, and they should be in open water for several hundred miles as they traveled east—almost until they were north of Cape Bathurst. With luck, if the weather held—and there was every likelihood that it would—he'd be able to remain on manual control for many hours before switching to the automatic navigation system and the dive under the ice. He picked up the telephone on the panel. Harding's voice answered from the control room.

"Fill forward and aft ballast tanks to half, repeat half," he said.

"Aye, aye, sir."

From the bridge lookout he watched the bow wave streaming aft. He heard the warning buzzer from the control room indicating that the tanks were filling. As the submarine settled deeper in the water the bow wave subsided and disappeared. The hatch automatically slammed shut. Millwood climbed down the ladder and took up a position behind Harding, who was intently watching the wall dials. The pointers on the gauges whirled around as the sea poured into the tanks. They steadied at the halfway mark. Millwood stepped in front of Harding and pushed the engine power lever forward. The RPM counter wound around the dial, until the speed indicator reached 30. At speed, Millwood tested his rudder response, left and right, then cut speed to 18 knots.

"She's more sluggish on the helm than the simulated tests showed," he said.

"That's caused by inertia from our heavy cargo, of course. We expected that," Harding observed.

"I didn't expect her to respond so slowly," Millwood said. "She's probably sluggish in the dive and surfacing modes too."

He glanced around to see what Eva was doing. She was at her position before the main electronics panel, watching a flickering cathode ray tube.

"Where's Simoncelli?" Millwood asked.

"In his cabin. He said he wanted to lie down."

"Check that he's secure before we practice a full-load dive."

"Yes, Captain." She hopped off her seat and went aft. While she was gone Millwood ran his eyes over the other instruments. He reached for the clipboard on the control desk and jotted down some figures. Eva reappeared. "He's fast asleep and tucked in safely, Captain."

"Stand by to dive." Millwood pushed a lever, the floor sloped, and the diving buzzer sounded. The clinometer on the instrument panel showed 10 degrees. He pushed harder, feeling the submarine's descent angle increase slowly under the pressure of his thumb. Twelve degrees, then 15. He pulled the lever back, but the clinometer hardly moved. After a few seconds the needle slowly centered, indicating that *North Star* had leveled off. He advanced the power lever until the indicator steadied at 23 knots.

"Fully submerged and steady as she goes. But slow to respond in the pitching plane."

"But at least we're going home faster than the *Manhattan and* with a full cargo of crude, sir," Harding said cheerfully.

Millwood smiled. "Stand by for surfacing."

"Standing by," Harding responded. Millwood moved the control and, after what seemed a long pause, the clinometer needle grudgingly shifted. A red light on the panel lazily changed to green, indicating they had surfaced.

"Eva, up antenna and signal Prudhoe."

"Yes, Captain."

She handed him the radiophone. He pressed the button. "Submarine tanker *North Star* to Prudhoe Bay. Are you receiving me? Over."

"Yes, Captain Millwood. We've got you. Over."

"We've dived under manual control with full load and have resurfaced. But the vessel is sluggish responding to helm and in dive and surfacing modes. Have you got that?"

"Yes, sir. Sluggish in helm, dive, and surfacing modes."

"Will you relay that information to Boston?"

"Yes, Captain. I sent your other message earlier. Mr. Blake gave it to me."

"Thanks. We're setting course due east. What's your maximum radio range?"

"About two hundred miles, Captain. But the aurora's been making our signal act up lately. It's been a terrific year for sunspots too, and they play hell on our wave band. If you want to give us a last message before diving, call us before the two-hundred-mile mark."

"Thanks. I will. Good-by for now."

Millwood moved the engine control knob forward until the knot indicator moved to 25. He felt the frequency of the engines' vibration under his feet increase, glanced at the RPM counter, and eased the power lever back a notch. The indicator hung at the 26 mark, climbed slowly to 28 and steadied on 36. "Good girl! I knew you could do it!" He winked at Eva. "It takes an old man to get the best performance out of a young lady!"

"You're not old, and you know it," she retorted. "Maybe you mean experienced sailor."

"Hi, there! Are we up or down? I never know with this ship." Simoncelli entered the control room, bracing his arms and yawning. "I just lay down for a stretch and must've dropped off. Where the hell are we?"

Millwood glanced at the position readout. "Coming up to two hundred miles from Prudhoe, loaded to the gunwales with oil. Hopefully at a delivery price that'll beat the pipeliners!"

"Humble Oil reckon they could save six hundred thousand bucks a day by crashing *Manhattan* through the Northwest Passage, so think what we can do at twice the speed!" Simoncelli was suddenly fully awake. "Humble Oil put up thirty-nine million bucks for *Manhattan,* with Atlantic Richfield and BP Oil kicking in another two million dollars each. That's big bananas, Frank. There's a million and a half bucks profit a *day* for oil companies holding Alaskan leases, if they can get the stuff to market at reasonable cost." He plunked his broad bottom against the golden barrel and heaved himself up. "Listen," he went on, in a confidential tone. "D'you think I'd get into this thing so deeply if I couldn't see the dollars and cents in it? I *know* we can deliver this oil"—he waved an unlit cigar through the air as he indicated *North Star*'s cargo —"for sixty cents a barrel profit in New York, eighty cents in Chicago, and if I had to ship it to Los Angeles I'd come up with a clear ninety cents a barrel profit." He stuck the cigar between his lips, struck a match, and applied it to the end of the cigar.

"By going through the Bering Strait instead of heading east?" asked Harding.

"Of course! Of course!" exclaimed Simoncelli, swinging his feet and thumping the heels of his boots against the barrel. He looked at Harding for a second or two, his big head slanted sideways, a quizzical expression on his face. "You didn't think *North Star* was limited to the Prudhoe-East Coast run, did you? With her range she can go around the world several times without refueling. Yes, sir!" He lowered a beefy hand and banged his knuckles against the metal barrel. "There's a hell of a market for oil in Tromsø, Norway. That's a bit more than two thousand miles from where we are now, I'd guess. Isn't that about it, Captain?" Simoncelli asked.

"About that. Actually——"

"And there's the rest of Europe: Britain, Germany, France, and there's Japan—"

"What about Middle East oil?" Harding interrupted.

"You'd have to be damn competitive to beat that, especially with transporting to the countries you mentioned." There was an undercurrent of doubt in his voice.

"Bull! We'll knock the hell out of Middle East prices. We've got the speed! By the time a supertanker got around the Cape of Good Hope with a single load, we could do three trips across the top of the world under the ice."

Millwood had often tried to estimate Simoncelli's age. He had to be at least seventy-five. His name had been famous in oil exploration before Millwood had even thought of joining the Navy. Oilmen did crazy things in those days. He remembered reading in the newspapers about Simoncelli's go-it-alone explorations in Alberta, and the great wildcat strike at Leduc from which he had returned to Houston a tough, two-fisted promoter with a majority interest in five wells. The rest was legendary: his hit-'em-hard gamble in the Yukon wells, followed by his financial wizardry in gaining multiple interests in North Slope oil. With his hold on Venezuelan crude and a major control of North Sea exploration, he had become the Oil King. Money flowed into his pockets as fast as oil was pumped out of the ground. Millwood tried to envisage him as a young man, with a wife and kids, but somehow the image didn't fit. There'd been a rumor of a scandal way back, with the daughter of a Greek shipping magnate, and of a vicious fight in which Simoncelli—a physically powerful man in his younger days—had been accused of murder. The affair had been hushed up, in the manner of the rich, but Simoncelli had always lived under a shadow among those who had remembered. As he turned to look at him now, Millwood couldn't visualize this six-foot husky man with the scarred face and the thatch of peppery hair worrying about a little scandal.

"Take a look now, Oscar," he said. "She's doing a hairbreadth over thirty-six knots and flat out!"

Simoncelli clambered off the barrel and stood at Millwood's side, legs spread in a commanding posture, staring through the lookout.

"That's beautiful, just beautiful!" he said, following Millwood's pointing finger. Millwood studied the bow wave as it foamed aft. The reflection of the midnight sun bounced off the polished foredeck. There was a slight sea running, and Millwood noted with satisfaction that the overcast was clearing. The Anchorage forecast had been dead on. He directed Harding to take over while he checked their position, keeping the ship headed due east.

He strode to the chart table, made a calculation, scribbled some figures on a piece of paper, and gave it to Eva. He was aware of the fragrance of her scent as he stood behind the chair. "What's your readout?" he said.

She read off their position, which corresponded exactly with the figures on the paper. He had the impression sometimes that she doted on the complex electronic equipment that had navigated *North Star* so unerringly below the ice. But then, she was something of a genius. Top honors from MIT, a brilliant thesis on an electronics navigation theory tied in with Einstein's theory of relativity, and a background in the Swedish Naval Academy. She had come to the United States eight years ago, after her husband had suddenly died. As he looked at her face with its pert nose, high cheekbones, and generous mouth, he guessed her age at around thirty-eight.

"Thanks," he said. "They jibe."

"Shows how accurate your navigation is, Captain," she replied agreeably.

Millwood considered for a moment before giving her instructions. "Run through your checks on the computer tapes.

Then stand by to engage the Auto Nav."

"Yes, Captain."

She leaned across to another console and selected a switch. Immediately two large television monitoring screens on the forward bulkhead of the control room glowed with a blue light. Scattered lines flickered across them and Millwood could see the faint shadows and highlights as the upward-beamed television camera on the submarine's deck picked up the wispy clouds overhead. After they dived the monitors would show the canopy of ice passing overhead, not unlike the slowly moving picture of the sky he now watched. Eva pressed a button and the pointers on two power-supply dials high over her head swung lazily through ninety-degree arcs and came to rest in the safety area.

"Everything's set, Captain. Ready to engage."

"Engage Auto Nav."

Eva pressed a button. The Auto Mode light lit up. She glanced at the computer cabinet at the back of the control room and instinctively Millwood's eyes followed hers. A panel at the top of the computer cabinet had lit up with the words "Transit Blue Locked On." *North Star*'s automatic navigation system was now responding to signals from the first of several sonar buoys anchored on the seabed far below the ice. They were going through the four transits in reverse order from their outward voyage. After "Transit Blue" would be "Transit White," between Banks Island and Victoria Island. Then would come the long "Transit Red," several thousand miles through Viscount Melville and Lancaster Sounds, the submarine unfailingly obeying the electronic buoys on the bottom sending their programmed signals to the Auto Nav system on board *North Star*. The last transit, "Transit Green," would take them into Baffin Bay and down to Cape Dyer, at which point, if the sea was ice-free, he'd switch off, surface, and proceed south to the New Jersey refinery port under manual control.

It wouldn't be long now before they came within range of the first buoy's signal that would automatically put *North Star* into a dive. As the vessel slid below the surface, the probing sonars on her upper deck would automatically feed signals to the computer and keep her at a safe distance below the ice by controlling the motors that operated the bow diving planes, the stubby winglike fins on each side of the hull. At the same time the downward-facing sonars would keep her from hitting the ocean floor, and the forward anti-collision sonars would guide her around such obstacles as the submerged portions of icebergs. Millwood wondered how much time there was before the dive signal. He had turned to ask Eva, when Simoncelli shouted, "Jesus Christ! Whales! A whole school of them!"

Harding leaped to Simoncelli's side. "Over there! Close up!" Simoncelli pointed with the cigar.

"Belugas," said Millwood over his shoulder. "There they go, over and under! There's supposed to be a lot in these northern waters."

Eva ran to the glass. "They're beautiful!" she exclaimed. "All white! They're not very big for whales. Are they babies?"

"They don't grow much bigger than ten feet," Millwood answered. "Sort of overgrown dolphins. The only time I've seen them was in the Gulf of St. Lawrence. Hey! Everybody back on duty!"

Simoncelli laughed. "Except me. I'll carry on as Captain Ahab!"

Millwood checked the sky. It was clear now except for a pale sepia stain to the south, where the Alaska coastline lay over the horizon. In the southwest, low in the sky, the midnight sun swung steadily through its Arctic orbit, lighting the sea with a burst of silver. He picked up the binoculars and intently studied the sky over *North Star*'s bow. Suddenly he pointed.

"The light under that distant cloud—a whitish glare below the horizon," he called to Harding. "That's ice blink. Beyond that we can expect heavy pack ice." He put down the binoculars and turned to Eva. "Give me an estimate of our running time until the Auto Nav goes to dive."

Eva moved a switch on the console, and numerals appeared in a readout panel. "Twenty minutes and eleven seconds to dive," she announced.

"That'll put us well below the surface before we come near the pack ice. Once we're below, we'll divide into our watches if Oscar'll take his usual stint in the galley . . ."

"Just say the word, Captain," Simoncelli said. "They used to call me the Yankee Camp Cook when I was a roughneck on the Yukon oil fields. But those dinners you got back there in the galley are precooked TV dinners. The company didn't mention *those* when they let me come on this cruise."

Millwood laughed. "You didn't mention the wine list, Oscar. That's not precooked!"

"Yeah! But what've you got in the thirst department besides rum and Coke and a bit of sherry? Herbert Armstrong knows I'm a bourbon man."

"He also knows the doctor told you to lay off. Nearly two weeks on the wagon is going to help your old ticker. That's the way I heard it." Millwood spoke with a quiet firmness, eyeing the cigar between the other's lips. He knew that if he insisted he could stop Simoncelli smoking too. But what the hell, he thought, you can't rob the old guy of all his earthly pleasures, not after the life he's lived. He moved back to the steering console, once more preoccupied by time, distance, speed, ice thicknesses, and depths of water.

He lifted the telephone on the console and pressed a button. "Engine room," Crane's gravelly voice sounded in the earpiece.

"We're diving in approximately twenty minutes. Any problems?"

"No, Captain."

"We'll divide into the same watches we arranged on the outward voyage after we're submerged," Millwood said. The division of watches had worked out well, he reflected, despite the fact there were only four of them. It had been a bit unorthodox from usual shipboard practice, with many six-hour instead of four-hour watches.

"Right, sir," Crane said. "Is there anything else, sir?" he added laconically.

"That's all," Millwood said, and replaced the receiver. Crane was a cool customer, he thought. He never said much. He wasn't unfriendly—it was simply his manner, reserved and quiet. Chosen for the voyage for his tremendous background in nuclear physics and marine engineering, he was a rare bird. He'd been an officer on several of the Navy's nuclear subs during their trans-Polar voyages under the ice and, like all the men aboard—with the exception of Simoncelli—was a reserve officer in the United States Navy. Eva was a special case: she belonged to the Navy's experimental electronics laboratories and had been seconded, after Simoncelli had pulled strings in Washington, to the consortium of oil companies—Prudhoe-Northwest Passage Corporation—that controlled and operated the *North Star* venture.

Millwood turned to Eva. "Try Prudhoe before we get out of their range," he said. "With this aurora interference we'd better not leave it too late."

"Yes, Captain." She reached forward and flicked the transmit switch.

"Submarine tanker *North Star* calling Prudhoe Bay." She

spoke quietly into the phone, at the same time switching on the overhead speakers.

"Prudhoe Bay receiving you loud and clear."

She handed the phone to Millwood. "Captain Millwood speaking. Please relay this information to Boston: We're on Auto Nav Mode—got that?—and will be diving in less than twenty minutes. The ice pack is now within eye contact. Inform Boston we'll contact them as soon as we surface somewhere in Baffin Bay in approximately three days. Tell them the exact time of our next transmission will depend on surfacing conditions off Baffin Island. Message understood?"

"Yes, sir. I'll relay it right away. Anything else, sir?"

"That's all."

"Oh—sir."

"Yes?"

"Everybody here wishes you the best of luck, sir."

"Thank you. Good-by." He handed the phone to Eva. "You can hang this up. We won't be needing it for a long time."

THREE

Millwood glanced at Eva's readout. Eighteen seconds to dive. Once more he ran his eye over the instruments as *North Star* raced across the surface of the sea. Two minutes ago the steel door in the sail had clanged shut under instructions from the electronic gear. Now, as he watched the digital readout flick over its numerals silently, he steadied himself for the downward movement.

"Everybody secure?" he asked quietly.

"Aye, aye, Captain," Harding replied.

He saw Eva give her seat belt a last-second tug. "Yes, Captain," she said. He glanced round at Simoncelli. The big man had braced himself near the periscope housing, his eyes glued to the monitoring screens, an expectant look on his face.

Millwood saw the digits change rapidly. Five seconds— four—three—two—one. A line of zeros lit up. For a second or two nothing happened. Then he felt the floor slope beneath his feet and heard the gurgle of distant water. The diving buzzer sounded briefly, cut out, and everything suddenly went quiet. He checked the monitors. They showed a pattern of swirls and eddies, which quickly cleared and grew light, until the screens glowed evenly. The clinometer showed 10 degrees, moved to 12, and steadied on 15, their steepest diving angle. He glanced at the depth gauge. The readout showed one hundred feet and increasing.

"Sonars responding?" he asked.

"Yes, Captain, All A-okay," Eva replied.

He grunted with satisfaction, and looked at the depth gauge again. As he did so the floor began to level off. The depth gauge slowed and hovered on the one-hundred-and-thirty-foot mark.

"She'll go deeper as we approach the ice canopy," he said. "The pack's about ten to twelve feet thick in these waters."

"Probably old ice that's been around for years," Harding remarked.

"Probably," Millwood agreed, his eyes still on the depth gauge. It had stabilized at one hundred and thirty five feet. He turned to Eva. "Check range to the ice. Your upward and forward probing sonar will show it now."

Eva pressed a button and consulted a cathode ray readout that lit up. "Four nautical miles, Captain."

"Call off the miles as we come up to it."

"Aye, aye, Captain."

"The water's clear," Simoncelli said, pointing to the monitors. Millwood gave them a quick look. The eddies had subsided and the screens showed pictures of the undersurface of the sea, splotchy as the television camera mounted on *North Star*'s deck picked up the surface waves.

"Three nautical miles, Captain," Eva announced.

He ran his eye around the instruments again. As he came to the RPM counters he wondered how Crane was getting on aft. He'd often thought on the outward voyage how lonely it must be for him on his inspection tours of the nuclear reactor, the engines, and the array of auxiliary equipment he guarded so jealously in his little kingdom near the aft radiation-proof bulkhead. He liked being on his own: once his duties in the control room were over he usually hurried aft to his turbines, condensers, and auxiliary gear.

"Two nautical miles."

He glanced at the depth gauge and a few seconds later felt the floor slope as the numerals started to tumble at a steady rate. One hundred and fifty . . . The floor started to level off. The figures slowed and stabilized on 200.

"Steady as she goes," he announced. "Depth two hundred feet. Course ninety degrees, east. Auto Nav in Transit Blue."

"And all's well, Captain," Eva said, smiling.

Millwood was surprised how quickly the first two days had passed. The homeward voyage somehow seemed shorter than the outward. It had always been like that, even during those damned dull voyages out to the Korean coast and on the patrols up and down the coast peering through the periscope for the stray enemy surface vessel. They never did spot any, and the Korean War, as far as he was concerned, had been a series of boring excursions viewing distant coastlines, interspersed with pleasant leaves in Japan with one outstanding bang-up holiday in Kyoto with Betty, who had flown out from the coast.

"Checkmate," he announced, sliding his bishop across the chessboard that Crane had set up in his little wardroom off the engine room. The high-pitched whine of the turbines and subdued hum of electric motors filled the room with background noise. For a moment he thought that Crane hadn't heard him.

"It's mate, I think," he said louder.

"You win again, Captain." Crane smiled glumly, putting the chessmen away. "How about another game next time you're off duty, sir?"

"It'll be a pleasure," Millwood said, smiling and taking his jacket from the hook on the wall. "You should have protected the bishop with your rook."

"I know," Crane said. "I'm weak on playing the bishops."

"I must get back to the control room. See you later," Millwood said.

Harding was diligently jotting down some figures onto a clipboard when he got back to the control room. Eva was also still on duty, sitting relaxed on her stool watching the cathode ray tube readout showing *North Star*'s position.

"Good morning, Captain," Harding said, looking up briefly. "It's another morning, according to the chronometer!"

"The third already," Millwood replied. "All goes well." He glanced at the lighted panel above the computer cabinet. It showed Transit Red, telling him the sub was in the long lap under Viscount Melville and Lancaster Sounds. He crossed to Eva's position and stood behind her. She looked up and smiled.

"What's our range to the next beacon?" he asked.

She pressed a button and figures flashed on a panel set back on her desk. "Two hundred and four nautical miles to the final beacon on Transit Red, Captain," she said.

He went to the table, bent over a chart and quickly checked their position.

"We're about halfway home," he said. "That'll make Mr. Simoncelli happy. Is he asleep?"

"The last time I saw him he was raiding the galley," Eva chuckled.

Millwood nodded at the panel that Eva had just switched off. "That puts us north of Bylot Island. We'll soon be making the turn into Transit Green—south into Baffin Bay and on our way to Cape Dyer."

"Somehow it seems shorter going home, Captain," Eva said.

44

"It's psychological. As far as my calculations show, the miles measure the same whether you're going from east to west or from west to east," he laughed.

"I met an old guy in the Navy who tried to convince me otherwise, Captain," Harding said. "He was a member of the Flat Earth Society and had me worried for a while in case the ship might fall off the edge of the Atlantic! He claimed a mile was slightly longer east to west on account of—"

"The undersurface of the ice must be getting irregular," Millwood interrupted, as the depth gauge started to make its characteristic pinging sound, indicating the sub had started to ascend. The gauge numerals turned over. His body, sensitized after years at sea in submarines, told him *North Star* was moving upward at an unusually steep angle compared to her normal trim correction maneuvering. He glanced at the clinometer. It showed a four-degree upward tilt. The upward-facing sonars, tracing their path along the undersurface of the ice, were responding to some sudden variation in the structure and formation of the ice. The monitoring screens were a dark gray: that was normal for their depth. The speed indicator showed 30 knots.

"Say, we *are* going up in a hurry."

The gauge showed 140 feet and the clinometer 6 degrees. He wondered if they were approaching a lead, or skylight— a sometimes navigable passage through the ice pack. The monitor screens were lighter now, indicating definitely thinner ice, but probably still too thick to surface if he wanted to radio a position report to Boston. From the outbound voyage, and from the reports of the Navy's atomic-powered *Nautilus* during her voyage under the ice to the North Pole, he expected to pass below many of these narrow pathways, some of which changed position with the massive drift of the northern ice while some, near the coastal regions, stayed in more or less the same location year after year. The official reports had been laced with the new vernacular of the Arctic submariners, including *polynyas*, large areas of open water surrounded by ice. The word was Russian, adopted by the United States under-ice explorers.

The pinging increased in tempo. They passed through one hundred feet below the surface, and Millwood reminded himself that the gauge, being a sonar-operated instrument, measured the exact distance from the vessel to the ice undersurface.

"Eighty feet, Captain!" Harding's voice sounded taut.

He felt the floor take an upward turn and jerked his head to check the clinometer. It showed 15 degrees, *North Star's* maximum surfacing angle.

"Sixty feet, Captain!"

The screens suddenly darkened, indicating very thick ice. He breathed easier, and waited to feel the floor level off and take a downward inclination as the automatic sonar system worked the sub's bow planes. But the clinometer needle clung to the 15-degree mark. For a long moment he stared at the needle, but it held fixedly to the maximum surfacing angle line as if it had been painted on the dial.

"Forty feet, Captain!"

The *ping-ping-ping* quickened. He glanced at the anti-collision sonarscope. At its center was a dark shape that suddenly blossomed outward, filling the screen.

"Sonar to Manual, Eva!" he shouted. He heard a click as Eva's hand shot out and a green light flashed on her console, indicating that the bow planes were unlocked from the electronic system. Grabbing the diving lever, he rammed it full forward.

"Thirty feet, Captain!" Harding called.

Millwood pressed the lever forward until it was hard

against its stop. With his other hand he yanked back the power lever. In a moment that would always be etched deeply in his consciousness he visualized the massive submarine gliding inexorably upward, her heavy liquid cargo thrusting her with colossal momentum toward the steel-hard ice canopy. His knuckles grew white.

"Twenty feet, Captain!"

The knots indicator fell to 26. He glanced at the clinometer. It moved grudgingly . . . 14 degrees . . . 13 . . . 12. . . .

"Ten feet, Cap——"

The last syllable was drowned out by a metallic clang that resounded dully through the vessel. He heard a distant brushing sound, as though something was scraping along the foredeck. As he instinctively ducked his head Millwood checked the clinometer. It was passing through zero and showing 2 degrees of Dive. Eva put her hands over her head as if to ward off a blow. Harding, gripping the edge of the control desk, stared at the ceiling. Millwood's eyes followed his; he waited tensely for the crash of water and steel plates buckling, and had a mental picture of millions of gallons of crude oil pouring into the control room, smothering them in black and green goo. The scraping sound ended, plunging the control room into a sudden silence.

A bellow of pain sounded from the aft quarters of the vessel.

"Harding! See who's hurt and report back."

"Aye, aye, Captain." Harding hurried aft.

The diving buzzer blared and the clinometer dropped to 5 degrees of Dive. He kept pressure on the diving lever and turned to Eva as she lifted her head from the console.

"It's all right. We're diving," he said, making a deliberate effort to keep his voice under control, aware of how flat and obvious he sounded.

47

He thrust the power lever forward as the clinometer passed through 10 degrees. The depth gauge showed 60 feet . . . 80. They passed through 100, continuing to dive.

"I don't understand, Captain. The sonar——"

"The automatic sonar kept the bow planes locked on maximum surfacing," Millwood interrupted.

Eva took a deep breath. "It didn't show up on my instruments." She stared at the console, a puzzled expression on her face. "I don't understand it," she repeated. "Theoretically, it couldn't happen."

"Well, it did," Millwood snapped, eyes on the instruments. He leveled *North Star* at two hundred feet and waited for her speed to come up. "It seemed like some sort of over-run. The bow planes were stuck at maximum surfacing." An old fear nagged him: although he accepted modern electronic equipment and had used the scientists' various magic black boxes for many years in submarines, nothing could quite dispel his latent distrust.

Harding hurried into the control room. "It's Mr. Simoncelli, Captain. He fell and broke his arm."

Millwood picked up the phone. "Crane . . . Yes, we struck the undersurface of the ice. Report to the control room immediately."

He replaced the phone. "We'll inspect the sail, Harding."

Crane entered the room, his face serious.

"Take the helm, Crane. Steady as she goes." He turned to Eva. "Go aft and attend to Mr. Simoncelli. You were a nurse once, I understand."

He saw Eva's eyebrows arch in surprise. This wasn't the time to explain that he'd read her professional career résumé with more than usual interest when she'd been seconded to *North Star*.

"Aye, aye, Captain," she said, moving toward the hatchway.

"Harding, follow me," he said, striding to the ladder and quickly climbing into the base of the sail. He ducked under the auxiliary steering panel.

"Take a close look around the foot of the sail structure. I'll check aloft." He reached overhead and flipped up the toggles that held a manhole-size hatch leading to the upper part of the sail. The hatch cover fell with a clang to the floor.

"You all right, Captain?" Harding called.

"It's only the hatch cover." Millwood put his hands up to grip the edge of the hole, but it was beyond reach. He jumped and caught the edges, wormed his body through the opening, and felt for a switch. Twin overhead lamps flooded light into the interior aerofoil section of the sail. He felt behind the broad periscope housing that passed from top to bottom of the sail and inspected the space between the radio antenna mounting, the snorkel, and the structure of the sail. No sign of moisture. Near the top of the sail were electric motors controlling the main access hatch. Quickly he looked for footing. Jamming his body against the steel skin of the sail, he gripped the housing and inched himself up, tearing a button from his jacket. He heard it make a sharp metallic sound as it dropped far below and cursed. By the time he was in line with the platform his face was covered with sweat. Probing with his hand, he felt in front of and behind the motors, then swept his fingers around the welded seam at the uppermost peak of the sail. Dry as a bone. Carefully he lowered himself until he stood on the floor of the sail.

"Any sign of damage?" he called through the hatch to Harding.

"No, Captain."

"Did you see a gold button fall down there?"

"No, Captain. But I'll look around."

He made a swift movement to check the sail again, switched out the lights, and climbed down the ladder.

"No button, Captain," Harding said, looking at the tuft of thread sticking out from Millwood's jacket. "What do you think happened?"

"The bow planes appeared to be over-riding. She responded only when I ordered Manual Mode but her weight kept her headed for the ice." He paused and looked overhead. "Replace that hatch," he said. While Harding reached up to throw the toggles he continued, "I think we hit some downward projecting outcrop of ice—maybe the bottom of an iceberg locked in the pack. If we'd hit the canopy we'd have damaged the sail." He paused again, thinking. "Yes, that's what happened. We struck an outcrop with one side of the bows, missing the sail completely."

"It didn't sound like a big bump," Harding said. "But you can't tell with a heavily loaded vessel like this, of course." He crinkled his forehead. "We won't be able to inspect the bows until we surface in Baffin Bay, Captain?"

"Not unless a big enough polynya shows up before then," Millwood replied, climbing down the ladder. In the control room he turned to Crane.

"Stand down, Crane. Harding'll take over."

"Aye, aye, sir."

"Crane, stand watch on the monitoring screens. I'm going aft to see what's happened to our passenger."

Simoncelli called out as he turned into the galley, "It's my goddamned arm! That's the third time I've broken it!" Eva had settled him in a chair, taken off his jacket, and rolled up his shirtsleeve. She had already made a temporary sling for the arm and applied a cold-water compress to an ugly bruise farther up the broken limb.

"Is it an open or closed break, Eva?" Millwood asked, inspecting the arm.

"I can't feel any bone ends, Captain."

Millwood pressed his fingers into the swollen flesh. He glanced at the old man's face. The rough-hewn features were impassive, but the ends of the lips quivered as Simoncelli fought the pain. "Feels like a closed break, Oscar. Can't be sure until you get it X-rayed."

"I know," Simoncelli growled irritably. "Now get it splinted up, will you, and stop making such a fuss."

Eva applied a splint and wound a broad bandage around it to secure it. She looked up at Millwood. "Would you mind tying the ends together, Captain, while I search in my cabin for a big safety pin? There doesn't seem to be one in this first-aid kit."

He tied the ends together as Eva hurried away.

"What happened?" he asked Simoncelli.

"I was fixing myself something to eat when the sub jerked and I lost my footing. I fell and got wedged between the freezer and the sink with my arm bent back. What the hell were you doing up front? Pretending to drive a roller coaster?"

"We were surfacing, but changed our minds and dived," Millwood lied.

"Surfacing, eh? Then it must be clear upstairs."

"We thought it was. But it wasn't. So at the last moment we dived. Sorry about this." He nodded at Simoncelli's arm.

Eva hurried back and eased the jacket over Simoncelli's shoulders. "Put your good arm through here," she instructed. She bent down to inspect the knot Millwood had tied.

"I wish I could tie a *flat* reef knot like that," she remarked, smiling.

"It takes an experienced sailor to tie one," Millwood said, grinning. "Electronics engineers only know about complicated things."

Eva slid the safety pin through the corduroy jacket.

"That'll take the weight," she said to Simoncelli, and put the things back into the first aid kit.

"Thanks very much," Simoncelli said, patting his arm with his free hand. He turned to Millwood. "Now, if you'll keep this ship on an even keel I'll finish fixing that ham sandwich!"

Eva had removed a panel covering the back of the console, exposing a mass of wires and junction boxes. She looked up at Millwood.

"I've checked out the sonar system. There's a short somewhere in the feedback circuit that controls the servo motor."

"The servo motor that operates the bow planes?" Harding asked.

"Yes. I can only test the primary circuits. The feedback circuit is considered a secondary circuit and requires special bulky testing equipment. It's usually done at the factory."

Millwood considered this for a moment. "The feedback instructs the servo motor when to stop?" he said.

Eva nodded. "That's correct. When it's working properly the feedback stops the motor immediately it senses the motor has moved the bow planes to the right position."

Millwood stroked his chin. "So the bow planes kept on tilting upward because the feedback signal from the servo motor was nonexistent. It had shorted out. That took the ship at an ever-increasing angle toward the surface until she was at her maximum surfacing angle of fifteen degrees." His mind returned to the question of hull damage. With *North Star*'s double outside skin and toughened steel construction she had probably suffered nothing more than some scraped paint from her bows. But now he'd have to keep her trimmed on an even keel under manual pitch control by using the diving lever. In temperate and tropical waters that was a safe and routine matter, but in polar seas, where sounding charts were often unreliable—nonexistent in some of the ice-covered regions they were traversing—there was a greater element of danger. The sooner they got *North Star* back under automatic pitch control the better.

He looked under his eyebrows at Eva. "It's up to you now," he said gravely.

She turned to him, and he saw the light at the back of her eyes. Her face was serious as she tossed her sandy hair and replied, "I understand, Captain."

Crane was watching the depth gauge and the engine power setting intently. "You can stand down, Crane. Harding'll take over."

"Aye, aye, sir," Crane said in his deep monotone. He added ruefully, "I guess this nixes our chess game, Captain."

"Afraid so. Until we get the automatic depth system fixed."

"I'll check the auxiliary gear, Captain. And I want to take a reading off the reactor output." He disappeared aft.

"Keep her at two hundred feet and full power, Harding. I'm going to get something to eat. Call me immediately if you notice anything abnormal. And keep an extra careful lookout on the anticollision sonar."

"Aye, aye, Captain."

Before he left the control room Millwood checked the monitoring screens. They were the usual gray, flecked with occasional streaks as *North Star* sped under narrow fissures in the ice canopy. In the galley he found Simoncelli eating a steak with gusto, stabbing the meat with a fork held in his unhurt hand.

"Jesus Christ, Oscar! You still stuffing yourself?" he grinned. "I thought you were fixing a ham sandwich." Inwardly he was pleased to see that his passenger had recovered enough from his ordeal to fix himself a substantial meal.

"Hi, Frank! Come and join me. I was hungrier for chow

than I thought. You seem to be on duty a hell of a long time. Everything all right up front?"

Simoncelli was nobody's fool. He noticed everything that went on in the running of the ship. It wouldn't take him long to find out about the faulty sonar system, so he might as well tell him.

"We're having a little trouble with the sonar system."

"What the hell's that? Oh—I know. That's like underwater radar. Lets you see ahead and up and down. Herbert explained it to me once."

"That's right. It failed to respond when we were adjusting our depth beneath some heavy ice. That's why we roller-coastered way back. When you broke your arm. Eva's trying to find the fault now." He stared at the splinted arm secured by Eva's safety pin to the big man's jacket. "How's the arm?"

"Oh, that," Simoncelli replied, barely glancing down. "Fine, Frank. After you've busted it three times you get used to it. Hey—how about something to eat? I've got a steak sizzling on the stove. By the way, I've got a suggestion to make if we go ahead with the other subs."

"What's that?"

"Make the stoves bigger. And add another cooking ring. It's awkward as hell trying to cook two steaks and mushrooms and keep the coffee hot all at the same time."

Millwood laughed. "You take the cake, Oscar! I'll make a note of your suggestion in my official report of the voyage."

"You'd better," Simoncelli said slyly. "Or I'll report *you* to Herbert!"

Millwood grinned and crossed to the stove. The steak was ready. He pushed it on to a plate, picked up a knife and fork, and sat down opposite Simoncelli.

"How is it?" Simoncelli said.

"Delicious. They didn't call you the Yankee Camp Cook

for nothing on the oil fields. I thought you said we only had precooked TV grub aboard. Where did you find these?"

"Oh, I dug around," the old man replied archly. "They were at the bottom of the freezer."

"You should've been a Navy cook," Millwood replied. "On second thought, after your stomach's been abused for a quarter century by guys claiming to be Navy cooks, I take that back. It's the tastiest steak I've had since coming aboard. With due respect," he added, glancing over his shoulder guiltily, "to our electronics engineer."

"She's pretty good," Simoncelli said magnanimously. "I had no complaints about the way she handled the chuck wagon on the outward journey." After a pause while he manipulated a toothpick, he said, "She's pretty smart, if you ask me."

"I hope she's as good an electronics repair expert as she is a cook," Millwood said thoughtfully.

"She'll fix it," Simoncelli said in a confidential tone. "I know her type. She's thorough." He nodded his head gravely. "There was a Swede woman working on the oil fields near San Antonio, a slip of a girl with a waist as thin as a wisp of hay." He dropped his fork and made a gripping motion with his broad hand. "She did the payroll and barrel-load accounts. I was young then and took a fancy to her, I don't mind admitting. She went over those accounts every day—we used to be paid by the day then—and was never a cent out. She did an exact check of every barrelful we pumped out of that ground, including spillage. Really thorough, I tell you." He bobbed his head up and down as he talked, and Millwood noticed for the first time that Simoncelli had no eyelashes. He'd wondered why the man's face seemed odd when he'd first met him in Boston. He made a mental note to ask Simoncelli about it one day; no doubt it would bring forth another tall tale from the oil fields. "You don't have to worry about *her*," Simoncelli finished, jerking his head toward the control room.

Millwood put his empty plate on the galley counter. "I'm just concerned about whether she can trace the fault and get the automatic sonar system working again." He helped himself to a generous portion of cheese, heaped some crackers on a plate, and sat down again.

"Look," Simoncelli said, eyes narrowing in concentration, "it's none of my business, Frank. I'm a passenger on this ship, and I came along for the ride, pure and simple. My ticket cost a hell of a lot of dough, if you consider my investment in this deal." He glanced around the room, a cell of steel enclosed in a larger capsule speeding through the dark waters beneath the polar ice. "So I felt entitled to see what I was buying. But that's by the way. What I'm saying is this: every man to his trade. You can't be an expert on everything these days. Look at me." Simoncelli swung out his good arm in an open gesture. "There's only one thing I know—and that's oil, and how to get the goddamned stuff out of the ground. If I want to know how to get the stuff across an ocean or a continent, I buy the services of someone who knows oil tankers or pipelines. Or an entirely new and cheaper way of doing it, like *North Star*. Money can buy everything: things, people—and brains. Now, I have a hunch you've got a brainy woman on board, and she'll fix that electronic contraption."

Simoncelli's wide face, etched deeply by tropical sun and cold northern winds, emanated confidence. Millwood studied the deep-set lashless eyes and marveled at the well-preserved head, the taut tendons beneath the skin of the tough neck. He relaxed, feeling that the burden had been shared with an experienced man wise in his knowledge of human nature. He also wondered if the old man's hunches about Eva included Millwood's ambivalent feelings toward her.

"Time for coffee," Simoncelli announced, getting up to fetch the pot. "Black as usual?"

"Thanks, yes. I'll take it to the control room. Give me one for Eva too."

He took the brimming mugs and went forward. Eva had folded the circuit diagrams and was probing with a screwdriver behind the back of the open computer cabinet.

"I brought you coffee," he said. "How's it going?"

She took a deep breath. "Just checking to see that nothing's shaken loose in here," she replied, nodding toward the cabinet. "I've seen the obvious happen before. A bad connection due to vibration or a carelessly soldered wire that somehow slips past final inspection."

Millwood took a sip of coffee. It hardly seemed likely that such a thing could happen with modern production methods, but he allowed her that much leeway. It was, he realised, her way of checking everything out from the ground up.

"And how did you find everything, Eva?"

She looked up at him. "Perfectly in order, Captain." She paused and added, "It's not a mechanical or electrical failure. At least not in here." She nodded toward the cabinet.

"What's your next step?"

"Trace the actual wiring—as much of it as I can in the control room. Obviously I can't check the wiring right out to the servo motors buried in the hull near the bow planes."

"That sounds logical, Eva. Carry on and report back when you've completed that phase."

"Yes, Captain."

Millwood crossed to the control desk. Harding looked up. "She keeps level very easily once you get her trimmed. On account of our weight and size."

"I'll take over. Simoncelli's discovered some super steaks buried in the freezer. If you go now you might easily persuade him to cook one for you," he grinned.

Harding looked pleased. "How's his arm, Captain?"

"He's okay. A tough bird. Claims it's the third time he's broken it."

"He's tough all right, Captain. And a nice guy." He turned to go, just as Simoncelli plodded into the control room with a dish towel and breadknife in his hand. "Anybody for grub? I've got a couple of steaks medium rare coming up." He stood in the hatchway, an expectant look on his face. Then he looked up toward the monitoring screens, and held the breadknife high, thrusting it like a rapier at the screens. "Look, Frank!"

Millwood jerked around and stared at the screens. They were solid black from edge to edge.

"Eva! Check to see if they're still switched on!" She ran to the console. "Switched on and locked, Captain."

"Then what the hell—!" Millwood blurted. "Christ! I hope the camera on deck is okay."

"Why shouldn't it be?" Harding asked. Millwood saw a thought dawn on his first officer's face before Harding voiced it. "Unless the ice——"

Eva interrupted. "The ice couldn't have damaged the camera. The circuit would show dead if it had." She pointed to the little signal light indicating that the circuit was alive. "But what *would* cause the screens to go solid black like that?"

The answer came to Millwood at the same time as it did to Eva. But it was she who spoke.

"It's oil, flowing over the camera lens! The ice must have damaged the bow after all." She turned to Millwood and, for the first time since he'd met her, he saw fear in her eyes.

FOUR

Millwood continued to stare at the screens. Blake's words shot through his brain: *If you want my opinion, it's more dangerous to ship sixty million gallons of crude oil under the ice, in spite of your safety systems.* Then his mind spun into action.

"Harding! In my cabin! The operational manual on the ship's structure. Fast!"

"Yes, Captain." Harding disappeared through the hatchway.

"Eva, if we stopped the leak somehow, would the camera aperture clear itself?" Millwood demanded.

Her delicate eyebrows formed two high arches. "It should clear at this speed, Captain." She shrugged and added, "It might leave a thin film over the lens. Distort the picture for a while. Nothing serious." He saw her fear recede as she forced herself to think logically.

Harding reappeared and placed a heavy book on the main control desk. Millwood turned to the section headed "Cargo Tanks and Oil Transfer System," and unfolded a diagram that showed *North Star*'s tanks and the complex piping system. There were four tanks the length of the vessel, built integrally with the hull. He studied the on-loading pipes, through which Blake's men had pumped the oil, and their control valves recessed in hatches. He knew that the only way oil could be withdrawn was at dockside after the submarine had berthed, when those valve hatches could be opened and special off-loading connections released the valves.

"The ice may have hit one of these," he said, putting a pencil point on the port and starboard valves. "Probably ripped the hatch cover off."

"Why, Captain?" Harding said.

"If it hit on the centerline the ice would have struck the sail, and we've already established it didn't do that."

"That makes sense," Harding said. Millwood looked up at the cargo tank gauges. The pointers had dropped. He wondered how long the oil had been leaking. It couldn't have been long or they would have noticed it on the darkened monitoring screens earlier.

"We've lost some cargo already." He had a mental picture of the oil streaming aft in a widening plume as *North Star* rushed under the ice, the dark liquid billowing toward the surface, spreading sideways in a flat black mat of semi-frozen goo trapped under the ice, forced by the action of the waves through leads in the ice pack. If he didn't stop the leak, *North Star* would leave a trail of oil hundreds of miles long through Lancaster Sound. It spelled disaster for the under-ice oil ferry project, to say nothing about the loss of sixty million gallons of oil to the company. Worse, it could lead to irreversible damage to the whole Arctic Sea area.

"We've *got* to stop that leak," he said, glaring at the dark screens. As he did so, the curtain of black parted and a flicker of light shone through. A gray pattern swirled against the screen, the oil plume eddying as it swept over the camera.

Millwood glanced at the sea temperature dial. The water

temperature had gone up 2 degrees. "There's the reason," he said, "we're passing through a warmer undercurrent."

"Why would that clear the screens?" asked Harding.

"I would hardly call that clearing," Eva interjected gloomily, watching the swirling pattern on the electronic picture tubes.

"The oil is rising faster in the warmer water. It's breaking clear before it covers the camera aperture completely," Millwood explained. It also meant that the oil was thinning and spreading over a wider area. The needles on the cargo tank gauges now showed a definite drop. The dials were calibrated in tens of thousands of gallons, with the total capacity indicated on each dial by a red line at the 30-million mark. The two integral tanks built into each side of the submarine were interconnected, an arrangement that allowed *North Star* to be loaded or unloaded from either side alone and remain on an even keel. This arrangement had a major disadvantage, Millwood realised now. All the oil *North Star* carried could ultimately be discharged through one leak. His mind raced on, analyzing the problem. There was no option open to him and he knew it.

Simoncelli was sitting on the golden barrel, staring at the screens, hypnotized by the black-and-gray picture of eddying oil. Millwood noticed deep pockets of fatigue under Harding's eyes. "Turn in for a spell," he told him.

"Okay, Captain." Harding sounded relieved, but appeared reluctant to leave the control room.

"You rest too, Eva. There's no point in us all wearing ourselves out. We can't stop the leak, at least not until we can surface and get at it. Take a spell off. The fault in the sonar system will have to remain for the time being."

Harding shuffled to the hatchway. "Shall I tell Crane to relieve you, Captain?"

Millwood shook his head. "No. I'm okay. If I need him I'll call."

Millwood checked the sub's position on the readout. They were beyond the point of no return—it made sense to press on. Once in Baffin Bay they'd be able to surface and radio for help.

Millwood waited for them to disappear and put a chair against the wall. He inspected the cargo gauges closely while Simoncelli silently watched from his perch on the barrel. The pointers on the gauges had dropped below the red lines. He peered at them, trying to estimate how much oil already had leaked. If the needles had dropped one percent of the distance between the small dots on the dial, that meant one thousand gallons had leaked from each tank. Four thousand gallons gone already. He got off the chair and scribbled down some figures. *North Star* would leak millions of gallons of oil in a sweeping crescent under the Arctic water surface, a spill that might feasibly drift south into the North Atlantic, crossing shipping lanes leading into New York and well-traveled East Coast ports. What if the oil leaked faster? He shuddered and looked at Simoncelli. The old man regarded him with cool eyes.

"It's bad, isn't it, Frank?" he said.

Millwood nodded.

Simoncelli tapped his fingers on the oil drum. "This damned voyage is jinxed."

Millwood wondered how much oil had pushed through to the upper surface of the ice. When the ice became looser, as it did at some points in the Polar seas, the crude would be squeezed between the floes and crevasses by wave action. How far out on the surface would it spread? Would the cold air congeal it and slow it down?

He glanced at the navigation readout and saw that they

were at the end of Transit Red. In a few moments the vessel would change course south-east as she maneuvered around the north of Baffin Island. He recalled the navigation reports that spoke of ice that piled up high as the currents swung them into the main channel through the Arctic Archipelago.

"Get off that barrel and sit tight, Oscar. There'll be a course change in a moment."

Simoncelli clambered off the barrel and sat in Eva's chair, holding on to the console with his left hand.

The navigation readout swung toward a southerly heading. "There she goes! Steady on eleven degrees east of due south." Surprisingly, the move into the new course was so smooth Millwood could hardly feel the pressure on the side of the seat. He turned to the panel on top of the computer cabinet. As he did so the Transit Red lazily changed to Transit Green. They were on the final long lap home.

"I think the oil's leaking faster!" Simoncelli exclaimed.

Millwood examined the cargo gauges. The pointers were lower.

"Frank. Level with me. How serious is it?" Simoncelli asked, his deep-set eyes searching Millwood's face.

"There's nothing we can do to stop it leaking."

"What the hell does that mean?"

Millwood shrugged. When he spoke his voice had a hard quality he did not recognize. "It means we are in the process of creating an oil spill across the top of the world, from Lancaster Sound down through Baffin Bay." He paused and went on deliberately. "And if we don't surface soon, we'll run the spill south through Davis Strait, where it will flow past Newfoundland, Maine, Massachusetts and—God, do I have to spell it out, Oscar?"

He wondered if planes flying their polar routes had spotted the spill. There would be much aircraft movement this time of year: Hercules transports freighting supplies to oil exploration and drilling rigs in the Arctic Islands, bush planes dropping into Eskimo settlements, and planes from the U.S. Strategic Air Command, directed from the War Room at Omaha, on their regular electronic spying missions, probing Russian radar signals from the East Siberian Sea to Novaya Zemlya. There'd be the commercial airline flights, too, on their polar routes between the Orient and Europe.

Simoncelli looked at the floor, his wide mouth open. His boisterous spirits had affected them all; he was a joy to have aboard. And now he'd let the old man down.

He moved his eyes to the monitoring screens and his mouth dropped open. The screens had suddenly changed from jet black to bright white!

"A polynya!" he cried, and instinctively put one hand on the engine power lever and the other on the telephone. But his reason told him to do nothing until there was a definite sign that the sea lake was big enough in which to surface safely. There was another important factor to bear in mind: even if he cut power *North Star*, with her massive momentum, would take at least five sea miles to come to a speed low enough for him to safely apply rudder, after switching off the Auto Nav, and come about in a full one-hundred-and-eighty-degree turn to get back to the polynya.

"Can we go up?" Simoncelli demanded.

"I hope so!"

The screens suddenly reverted to their dull black color. "God damn it!" Millwood said loudly.

Simoncelli snorted. "Like a wildcatter! Drill for months and wait and just as you give up hope the hole blows its top. You bust your ass getting the spout under control and the damned thing dies on you. Not a drop, not a drip!"

Millwood picked up the telephone and dialed a number. It rang several times before a tired voice answered. "First Officer Harding."

"Captain speaking. Report to the control room immediately."

He dialed another number. "Eva, report to the control room immediately." He was about to replace the receiver but changed his mind and added, "Sorry—it's urgent."

A half minute later they both appeared. "We've just passed under a polynya about three hundred yards long, at a guess. Big enough to surface in, with luck. We're going back on manual to find it." Millwood explained.

He waited for Eva to bend over her console. "Disengage Auto Nav."

She pushed a button. "Auto Nav disengaged, Captain." Millwood gripped the wheel that controlled *North Star*'s rudder. He turned to Harding. "Quarter speed ahead."

Millwood was glad to feel the control of the vessel in his own hands again and he waited impatiently for the knots indicator to drop. It seemed an age before the needle started to move and, when it did, it dropped sluggishly. He couldn't risk turning above eight knots. The crude oil would act like a huge centrifugal weight as it pressed toward the outside radius of the turn. He knew from her trials, when the simulated loads had been applied, that she had a tendency to yaw. He picked up the telephone again.

"Crane. I'm going to make a one-hundred-and-eighty-degree turn and am waiting for the power to fall off. Is there anything you can do to hurry things up?"

"Nothing, sir. I saw the power indicator flash. Are you cutting to zero, sir?"

"I want eight knots before turning."

"I'm afraid we'll have to wait for her way to fall off, sir."
Millwood silently cursed. "Report to the control room,"
he said. "We're going to attempt to surface."

The knots indicator dropped to 16 . . . 15 . . . 14. . . .
He impatiently drummed his fingers on the wheel's rim.
Twelve . . . 11. They must be miles past the polynya by
now. Ten . . . 9 . . . 8. He turned to Harding. "Steady on
eight knots."

"Eight knots it is, Captain."

Millwood swung the wheel, watching the turn indicator.
The pointer began to move. He felt the tilt as the vessel
changed course. His grip on the wheel tightened as he narrowed the turn, relaxed as he felt the floor shift at a steeper
angle under his feet. Impatiently he stared at the indicator
and then checked the gyro compass. They were swinging
steadily but their wide radius of turn was taking them farther
off course back to the polynya. Out of the corner of his eye
he saw Crane come into the control room, buttoning his
jacket. He stared at the screens before stationing himself
before an instrument panel near by.

"We just passed a small polynya," he explained. "We're
going back to find it."

Millwood watched the gyro compass swing through 90
degrees. The temptation to shove the power lever forward
to increase her speed mounted. *North Star* moved through
one hundred degrees. He imagined her wide sweep through
the dark waters, twin screws thrashing, rudder angled as he
held her steady. The compass continued its smooth turn.
One hundred and seventy degrees. He gripped the power
lever more firmly. As the vessel came up through 180 degrees
and the floor leveled he centered the wheel and pushed the
power lever forward to half speed.

"Harding—Crane—keep your eyes skinned on the screens for the polynya!"

"Aye, aye, sir," Crane said, turning to face the screens. Millwood glanced at the depth gauge. Two hundred feet. Although the screens were dark he could risk coming nearer the surface in preparation. The chance of an iceberg extending very deep below the ice in these waters was remote. He eased back the diving lever until the depth gauge showed 160. Eva must have felt the upward movement, for she looked around at him momentarily.

He was aware of the silence pressing in. A match flared as Simoncelli struggled to light a cigar with his good hand. Seconds went by. They grew into a minute—two minutes. At the end of five minutes his jaw sagged. He looked around. Everybody was in a frozen posture, poised like statues, staring at the black screens. The disappointment on their faces was undisguised.

"It must have closed up. Perhaps it's storming on the surface," he said almost apologetically. "That would shift the ice." He hardly believed it, and his voice sounded unconvincing even to himself. What had probably happened was that they were in a current and had drifted off course. Now what was he to do? Make another full turn and resume course? Switch back to Auto Nav and continue into Baffin Bay, and in the process continue to pollute the northern waters with the mucky crude until he surfaced? Or attempt to surface through the ice right now?

A quick check of the cargo gauges decided the matter for him. They showed that *North Star* had poured several hundred thousand gallons of the oil into the under-ice environment: there was no time to make a more accurate estimate.

"Stand by to surface!"

"Through the ice——?" Eva swung around. She bit her lip before turning back to the console.

"Harding, stand by to blow ballast. Crane, check power settings."

"Aye, aye, Captain."

Millwood pulled the power lever to quarter speed. As the knots fell off he moved it to slow.

"Crane, take over power."

"Aye, aye, sir."

Millwood moved aside to allow Crane to handle the engines. He glanced at the warning light indicating that the periscope and snorkel tube were down and locked. Even a trace of either extending beyond the top of the sail would cause irreparable damage while he probed the ice with the top of the sail.

They were slowing down rapidly now. The knots indicator showed 8 . . . 7 . . . 6. . . . *North Star* was coasting to a stop one hundred and fifty feet beneath the ice-covered sea. The needle sagged and rested on the zero mark.

"Stopped dead," Crane announced in a sepulchral voice.

"Harding. Commence blowing fore and aft ballast tanks at their slowest speed," Millwood said.

Millwood fastened his eyes on the depth gauge as the numerals rotated. One hundred and twenty . . . 110. . . . A *ping-ping-ping* sang out.

Up a notch, Harding!"

Harding twisted the knob. The depth gauge numerals clicked faster.

Millwood glanced at the monitoring screens and grunted. They were dark. He'd expected them to lighten as *North Star* approached the ice, but now oil from the ruptured bow was hovering in great pools above deck.

"We'll have to feel for it, Captain," Harding said.

The depth gauge showed 90 feet.

"Back a notch, Harding!" He saw Harding reach out and turn the knob. Better, he thought; but the gauge showed them rising too fast for safety. "Reverse ballast pumps," Millwood called.

Harding flipped off the main switch and moved another. Slowly the submarine's rate of ascent diminished. The numerals on the depth gauge turned over lazily.

"Cut!"

The numerals slowed and stopped on 75 feet. There was silence in the control room as *North Star* hung poised at her point of neutral buoyancy. He heard Simoncelli's heavy breathing.

"Up one," he said. Powerful electric pumps shot water from the ballast tanks. Millwood moved his eye to the gauge. Seventy feet . . . 69 . . . 68. . . .

"Hold!"

It was bad enough trying to surface blind in ordinary seas, but this groping for solid ice was infinitely worse. Suddenly the upward-facing sonar pinged erratically. "Uneven obstacle directly overhead, Captain," Eva said.

"Cut ballast tank pumps."

Harding's hand shot forward and twisted the knob.

The depth gauge showed 57 feet between the top of the sail and whatever lay above them. The erratic pinging puzzled him.

"Eva, check out the depth gauge."

He watched her finger depress a key and a green light lit up on a panel above the console. "Checks A-okay, Captain."

"Another outcropping of ice?" suggested Harding.

"That wouldn't make the pinging erratic when we're stationary," Millwood said. "Unless its lower surface was indented with big holes and cavities." He shook his head and sucked the corner of his lip thoughtfully.

"Switch to the first notch."

"Aye, aye, sir."

Again the upward sounding depth gauge slowly turned. Millwood felt tension build as the numerals ran down: 47 . . . 45 . . . 43. . . . Harding's hand strained as he gripped the control. Thirty-three . . . 31 . . . 29. . . .

"Cut!"

The hand relaxed. The depth gauge decelerated. The vessel's upward drift slowed and the gauge stopped halfway between 20 and 19 feet. The gauge sang out a rapid *ping-ping-ping-ping*. Millwood could feel sweat trickling down his forehead, and was about to raise a hand to wipe it when the pinging altered its beat. It was as if the electronic beam had intercepted a school of darting fish. Then the pinging grew even more irregular. He rubbed his chin with the ends of his fingers, and turned to the compass. It was swinging wildly.

"We're in a current! Quarter speed ahead, Crane!" he shouted.

Crane rammed the engine power levers through the notches. "Starboard five degrees!" Millwood called as the compass continued to swing. "Steady as she goes!" He waited for *North Star* to make way against the undertow, trying to estimate its strength. Deep vibration under his feet told of the engines straining to overcome the inertia of the vessel and her cargo. The needle slowly climbed to 8 knots.

"Quarter speed ahead, sir," said Crane. The gyrations of the compass slowed and finally steadied on northwest.

"Right rudder to one-three-five—steady, a little at a time," instructed Millwood.

Harding eased the wheel slowly. "Course due east at eight knots, sir," he finally reported.

"What happened?" asked Simoncelli.

"When we stopped we were in a turbulent current. It spun us as it carried us."

"I see that. But why the crazy pinging?"

"The sonar was picking up deep irregularities in the under-surface of the ice as we passed beneath it. "Frankly—" he broke off. He hadn't expected the undersurface to be so rough. Normally, young sea ice formed very quickly as the temperature dropped and had smooth upper and lower surfaces. He didn't like it. The ice above was old, hardened by several seasons of polar deep freeze until it was as tough as steel.

"We'll have to surface at another spot. Take her down to one hundred feet, Harding."

Harding pushed the diving lever until the depth gauge showed 100. Again Millwood visualized the thick black oil spreading out under the ice. The oil leak was an oppressive, unchangeable fact.

"When we try surfacing again, close the throttles at the last moment, when we get to twenty-five feet below the ice. That will help counteract any current drift."

"Aye, aye, sir," Crane replied.

Harding eased back the diving lever and Millwood stared at the numerals tumbling around the depth gauge. The numerals slowed. The pinging increased in frequency.

"Twenty-five it is, Captain," Harding said.

"Close throttles."

"Throttles closed, sir," said Crane.

"Blow ballast tanks on the first notch!"

The depth gauge began to move—20 feet . . . 19 . . . 15 . . . 13 . . . 9. The pinging was as constant as a tap dripping. Seven feet . . . 6 . . . 5. . . . The speed indicator showed the vessel was still coasting at 2 knots.

Millwood had a mental picture of *North Star* gliding slowly and silently along with the tip of her sail five feet below the ice surface. The indicator needle dropped, hovered, and fell to 1 knot, then came to rest at zero.

"Ballast! First notch!"

Harding turned the knob. Abruptly the steel sail crunched against a solid wall of ice. For a few seconds a distant grinding filled the room. Then came a deeper rumbling as the sail began to break through. For a long moment Millwood thought the vessel hadn't enough buoyancy to penetrate. A thunderous crash echoed through the ship, followed by silence.

"We made it, Captain," Eva said, exhaling in relief.

Millwood smiled. "Up scope, Harding!" he said, suppressing his excitement. Harding pressed the button. The raising gear whined. Harding stood aside for Millwood, who pressed his eyes to the glass. He stared at a chunk of ice as big as a two-story building. Rapidly he swung the periscope around and saw the ice field spreading to the horizon under a cloudy sky. In the near distance were other massive edifices of ice; close to *North Star*'s hull were smaller hummocks, smooth and blueish—ice leached clean of salt. Slowly he rotated the scope to the south. Barely two hundred yards away was the edge of a large polynya, whose ruffled waters surged under the action of a moderate to strong wind. The encircling ice of the distant shore was about a half-mile away. He suppressed his feelings and said, "Take a look, Harding!"

Harding clapped his eyes to the glass and started. "Hell! What a goddamn miss, sir!"

Eva peered into the glass. "Oh, Captain!" she exclaimed. She stepped aside, and Simoncelli put his big face to the glass. "Missed it by a gnat's eyebrow." He looked up at Millwood. "But the lake we passed was quite small."

Millwood took another look through the eyepiece and rotated the scope. "We passed under a finger of the polynya that sticks out on the southern end," he said. "If we'd been about a quarter mile north we'd have seen how big the polynya really is and surfaced with no problem." He straightened up, and Simoncelli took another peek through the glass. "Say! We've got company!" he exclaimed.

Millwood bent forward to the glass. A hundred yards away were two polar bears, swimming line astern, headed in their direction, heads raised inquisitively. He could see their open mouths and shining black eyes as they approached. They clambered onto the edge of the ice, flicked the water from their shoulders, and rose on their hindlegs.

"What is it?" Eva asked.

"Polar bears, having a friendly boxing match. Here, take a look."

When Millwood reclaimed the scope the bears were ambling away from *North Star*, ignoring the strange blue-gray shape projecting through the ice. Their gleaming white coats merged into the ice field, and soon they were faint white smudges moving among the distant ice hummocks.

Millwood looked up from the scope. "Eva. Get that antenna up."

Eva crossed to the console and moved a switch. Millwood stood behind her. "Try Boston," he said. "If we're out of range try to raise one of the Dewline stations. They can relay our signal."

He watched her switch on the radio power and tune the wave band. A heartening, familiar hum filled the air from the overhead speakers. "Submarine tanker *North Star* calling Prudhoe-Northwest Passage Corporation head office, Boston," she said, "Come in, Boston." Only the hum broke the silence in the control room.

"I'll check the book," she said, searching the bookshelf. She took down a slim volume. "There's a Dewline station up here——"

"Try Boston again first," Millwood said.

She did as he asked, but again, only the hum.

"Harding, get the snorkel up." Millwood wondered why he hadn't ordered it raised before. The room was flooded with cool fresh air.

Eva turned the pages and located the nearest Dewline station. "There's one not far from Arctic Bay, on the northern tip of Baffin Island, Captain."

"Call them. You've got the call sign?"

"Yes, Captain." She spoke the call signal. "Submarine tanker *North Star* . . . Come in Dewline base."

Silence. Suddenly a flat, cracking sound resounded through the hull. Simoncelli looked up, startled. "It's the ice contracting," Millwood said reassuringly. "Call again."

The speakers remained silent. Then as Eva picked up the radiophone a distant voice sounded through the speakers. "Hello . . . Submarine tanker *North Star*. Are you receiving me?" It was a coarse voice, like one of the roughnecks at Prudhoe.

"Yes, Dewline base. We are receiving you. But faintly."

"This isn't a Dewline base. It's Baker Lake, Northwest Territories. I got you by accident. I check the airwaves when I'm off duty. Never know what you might pick up. Are you pretty?"

Eva clasped the instrument tighter. "I hear you better now."

Millwood ran to the chart table and hunted for a map of northern Canada. Baker Lake was about a thousand miles away. Some freak of transmission had got them a mining camp. "Eva, ask him if he can get Boston from where he is."

"Hello, Baker Lake. Can you relay a message to Boston, Massachusetts?"

74

"Sure, anything for a pretty girl. I sometimes pick up Boston through a microwave link to Frobisher Bay in Baffin Island. What d'you want me to tell them?"

Eva turned to Millwood.

"Give him our position. Harding, write it down for her. And tell him to let Boston know we're in distress. Leaking oil and surfaced through the ice." Harding scribbled down some figures and handed a piece of paper to Eva. She repeated them for the unknown man so far away.

He answered at once. "Got it, miss. I'll contact them right away. Stand by."

Millwood gazed at the now silent radio. They were lucky. It might have taken longer to make radio contact, considering the queer atmospherics caused by the aurora and northern magnetic fields. Suddenly the radio crackled and the voice came on again.

"Boston says to stay on the surface. They've checked your position and will arrange to send a salvage ship. Wow! They wouldn't believe me when I told them it was you. They said to stay—repeat stay—on the surface, and to contact me on this wave band every hour. Anything else you want me to relay? Say, what's your name?"

Millwood stepped forward and took the instrument from Eva's grasp. "This is Captain Millwood speaking. When can we expect a rescue ship?" he demanded. "Relay the question to Boston."

He waited impatiently for the reply. Simoncelli was beaming, patting Eva on the back as she smiled happily. Now he realized under what terrible strain they'd all been living. Consciously, in their own way, each of them had controlled a personal fear and got on with the job of sailing the vessel.

"Baker Lake to *North Star*. Boston says it'll take about four days to get a rescue ship to you. They've got to get an icebreaker too. But they're going to get a helicopter up from one of the Dewline bases. Within the next three or four hours. It depends on the weather. They'll bring some oil experts, sir. And take your crew off if you want. Anything else?"

"No. Except to thank you very much. What's your name?"

"MacDonald, sir. But the folks in this godforsaken hole call me Randy. Don't ask why!"

Millwood suppressed a chuckle. "We'll contact you in one hour. Good-by—and thanks again, MacDonald." To Eva he said, "Make sure you've got his frequency."

"I've got it. How could I forget the number of such a lovesick swain?"

Millwood laughed. "Harding, follow me and we'll take a look topside."

He selected a button in the sail and pressed it. The whirr of an electric motor sounded, but the hatch, which normally slid open so effortlessly, screeched loudly on its rails.

"What the hell! It's jammed!" he said. He gave the steel hatch a clout with his shoe and, to his satisfaction, it suddenly slid back. Facing him was a block of ice as big as an oil drum, with light filtering around the edges.

"Get a crowbar, Harding."

"Aye, Captain." While Harding was away he pressed his face to the ice. He felt its stinging coldness on his cheek.

He helped Harding push the crowbar through the hatch, and the ice teetered on the platform steps and fell on deck with a metallic thump. A rush of cold air entered the sail. Peering out, Millwood saw *North Star*'s deck deep in great blocks of ice. At the starboard bow he saw the dark gleam of oil under the lip of the ice where the deck had partially broken through. He pointed to the spreading stain. "The bow didn't break through!"

"We came up too slowly, Captain. The round-down on the forward deck is still under water."

Millwood took a step onto the platform and turned toward the north. "The polynya! It's covered with oil!" he cried. His cry brought Crane, Eva and Simoncelli scrambling through the sail and on to the platform. He pointed to the black waters of the sea-lake a mere two hundred yards away, and smelled the pungent odor carried on the breeze.

"We've got to get down there and fix that leak!"

"Look!" Eva cried.

Millwood swung around and gave a horrified gasp. At the edge of the spreading oil were two black humps. The polar bears! They splashed with clumsy, painful movements toward the clear water.

"Can't you stuff something into the hole to stop the leak, Frank?" Simoncelli said.

Millwood considered. They'd have to lever the thick ice chunks off the round-down at the bow to get to the hole in the hull. They'd need to work with lifelines. On the other hand, if they submerged and came up inside the polynya the rupture would be exposed above the waterline. That seemed the best thing to do, although the deck would become covered with crude from the oily water.

Instinctively he looked at the sky. An ominous darkness had swept down from the northeast. Thin gray clouds scudded overhead, and he detected a movement in *North Star* as the ice around her shifted and she began to respond to the lift and heft of a distant weather disturbance. A storm was brewing, one of those blizzards he'd heard about that blow suddenly across the top of Baffin Bay, driven before a full nor'-easter. He cautiously stepped down to the deck and looked intently at the layers of ice heaped up on each side of *North*

Star. He heard Eva call a warning. The ice *was* moving, making clunking noises against the vessel's plates. Farther out, beyond the narrow leads, oil splashed over the ice, black stains splotching on the ice hummocks. He hurried to the platform as the quick bite of an icy wind nipped his face. He checked his watch. They couldn't submerge now: the helicopter would miss them—if it *could* get to them before the storm closed in. And there was that hourly radio signal he had to make to Baker Lake for relaying to Boston. He *must* stick it out on the surface. "Everybody below," he said, "except you, Harding."

In less than an hour the full storm was on them. From across the polynya a mass of water moved forward, its leading edge a wall of ice and foam. As it raced across the open water it gathered up oil, turning its creamy crest black. It crashed with a roar on the ice field, sending up a curtain of oily spray as a sudden onslaught of wind tore off Millwood's cap.

"Quick, Harding! Under cover!" he roared. He felt the slimy blods hit his head, and he passed his hand across his face, aware that he was making the mess worse. As the spray subsided he looked up. Harding had scrambled into the bridge. Flakes of snow started to fall, quickly turning to sleet. A resounding crack reverberated through the deck as he looked down at *North Star's* side.

Harding yelled from the hatch. He grasped the rail, slippery with oil, lost his footing, and fell. A sudden fear that he would be swept overboard gripped his stomach. Harding crept from the hatch, lowered himself down the steps, and Millwood felt the firm grasp of his hand. Regaining his footing, he crouched low and clambered up the steps and through the hatch.

"That was close," he said, brushing his clothes. "Shut the hatch. We'll have to submerge and wait until the storm blows itself out."

"We'll miss the helicopter, Captain."

Millwood shrugged. "We can't risk the ship in this ice. And the polynya may close up, so we can't try to ride it out there."

As he climbed into the control room the groaning and shrieking of the ice grinding against the vessel's side was deafening. Millwood knew it would be only a matter of minutes before the plates would buckle. And there were the bow diving planes to consider. If they were damaged they'd be in serious trouble.

"Eva! Radio Baker Lake and tell them we're submerging because of a severe storm and will surface in two hours if it's over by then." He had to shout to make himself heard over the noise. Inside the hull it sounded as if *North Star* was being dragged over a huge gravel bed.

"Down scope and snorkel, Harding. Prepare to submerge." He waited until Eva had spoken into the radiophone and put the instrument down. She nodded.

"Submerge!" he yelled.

A sudden crash sounded directly above the ceiling, as though big chunks of ice had fallen on deck. Simoncelli ducked. The icy world that surrounded them was a savage, roaring animal reluctant to let them out of its grasp. Eva sat at her console and stared at the ceiling. Millwood watched the depth gauge, fearing that *North Star* would be unable to shake free from the ice. The gauge stood at a prolonged zero, then the numerals began to decline rapidly. They were submerging! The thundering noises were left above, and in a minute the only sound was Simoncelli's heavy breathing. Millwood turned around.

"All right, Oscar. You can get off the floor now!"

"Better check out your face, Frank! Looks like you fell into a gasoline pit," Simoncelli retorted.

FIVE

Millwood woke, stretched, and looked at his watch. It was an hour since they'd submerged. He'd grudgingly taken the opportunity to catch up on much wanted sleep, leaving Harding and Eva on duty in the control room. Now it was time to attempt to surface again, hoping that the storm had blown over or at least abated enough for them to be able to keep a lookout for the helicopter. He got up from the bunk and put on his jacket, fumbling for the top button before he sleepily remembered it had been torn off.

In the control room Harding was keeping the submarine on station by referring to the gyro compass and operating the controls accordingly. He was surprised to see Eva standing on top of the computer cabinet and stretching her arms to the ceiling, where she'd unlocked the hinged lids of several conduit boxes.

"What's going on?" Millwood demanded.

Eva looked down. "I'm tracing the wires for the automatic sonar system, Captain. I've got a hunch the problem's definitely somewhere in the secondary wiring system."

"An electrical rather than an electronics fault?"

She shrugged. "The electronics section checks out, Captain. I'm convinced it's some electrical problem."

"Leave it now, Eva. We're going to try to surface."

"Aye, aye, Captain."

He waited until she'd snapped shut the conduit boxes and jumped down.

"Where're Crane and Mr. Simoncelli, Harding?"

"Officer Crane's aft, Captain. Mr. Simoncelli was fast asleep when I checked about ten minutes ago."

"We'll let him rest," Millwood said, picking up the telephone and dialing. "We're going to surface, Crane. Stand by."

He replaced the instrument and turned to Harding. "Stand by for surfacing." The depth gauge was at two hundred and fifty feet and the position indicator showed no change in their position since they'd dived. Harding had done a good job.

He checked the monitoring screens. They were dark gray.

"We'll move north a quarter mile. That should put us directly under the middle of the polynya," he said. "I'll take over, Harding."

He grasped the controls as Harding moved from the desk, applied power, and waited. The knots indicator edged up. At three knots he turned the wheel right, then left, his eye glued to the monitoring screens. They remained dark gray. A sinking feeling gripped his stomach.

"It seems to have disappeared, Captain. I kept her exactly on station."

"I know you did, Harding." He paused, staring at the screens as he rotated the wheel again, taking *North Star* on a zig-zag course at slow speed. "Hell! The storm must have closed the goddamned thing up tighter than a drum!" Again he twisted the wheel, but the screens remained dark.

"There's nothing to do but to surface through the ice again," he said, shutting off power. He waited for *North Star* to come to a stop.

"Blow ballast tanks, first notch."

"First notch it is, Captain," Harding replied.

Millwood looked at the depth gauge as the numerals rotated slowly. The pinging started. At one hundred and fifty feet he felt a slight tremor, as though *North Star* had found another sub-surface current. Harding didn't appear to have noticed it: he was peering at the depth gauge, hand gripping the ballast tank control. Again there was a tremor and this time Harding looked across at Millwood, but said nothing.

At ninety feet the ship shuddered again, this time so violently that the movement passed through the control room and dissipated somewhere aft. Then came a distant crash and grinding sound.

The depth gauge figures slowed and hovered on the 65 mark while *North Star* swayed. If he went higher they'd be knocked around by broken ice slabs.

"It's still storming up there. Cut ballast, Harding." He wondered how much oil had leaked during their enforced wait below. The cargo gauge pointers looked ominously lower. If he dived again and stayed below for another hour the storm might still be raging when he resurfaced, and during that hour still more oil would leak. There was no way of even guessing when the storm would blow itself out. It might go on for six hours, even as much as twelve. On the other hand, if they continued their voyage submerged they'd still lose oil, but there was a chance of surfacing farther down the coast of Baffin Island, out of range of the effects of the storm. He made a decision.

"Recharge ballast tanks, Harding. We'll submerge and press on."

Eva climbed back on top of the computer cabinet and undid the conduit box lids with a screwdriver. Millwood watched in silence as she traced the wiring until she came to a big panel built into the ceiling structure. She proceeded to undo the lid. As it swung down he saw a maze of thin colored wires bundled in neat harnesses.

"The main distribution box for the automatic sonar system?"

"Yes, Captain."

He swung around as Simoncelli plodded into the control room, yawning loudly. "Ah—that was a good rest," the old man exclaimed. He stared up at Eva. "Say, what's going on?"

"Eva has a hunch she knows where the sonar trouble is."

"Hey, Captain! I think it *is* here!" Eva yelled. "Look at this yellow wire. The insulation's rubbed right through! Yellow's the feedback circuit for the servo motors. It's shorted right out!"

She delicately eased a thin wire from the depths of the main distribution box. Millwood stood on tiptoe. The insulation had been worn right through, the strands of bare wire gleaming under the ceiling lights.

"How the hell would a thing like that happen? Harding, bring me a step ladder from aft. I'll take over while you're gone."

"Aye, aye, Captain."

When Harding reappeared with the ladder Millwood climbed to the ceiling next to Eva. The harnesses were tightly packed, each carefully bound in plastic clips, the whole contained in the metal distribution box welded to the steel structure. On the other side of the ceiling, he knew, were tons of cargo oil. A thought flashed through his mind. Supposing the pressure of oil had exerted weight on the ceiling structure and distorted the box, pinched the wires?—they were packed in really tight. But the ceiling structure was toughened steel. He raised his hand, gently pushed it through the maze of wires, and rested his palm on the base of the distribution box.

"Hey!" he exclaimed.

"What, Captain?" Eva asked.

"I can feel a strong engine vibration." The vibration plus the distortion of the base of the distribution box had rubbed the wire bare. "It chafed the wire," he said.

"Engineers call it a fretting action, sir," Crane, who had silently entered the control room, called up.

"Yes, I've heard them call it that. All this complex circuitry and sophisticated machinery knocked out by a little fretting!" Millwood said. He turned to Eva. "Well, your hunch was right," he said, smiling.

"I told you, Frank," Simoncelli said in a loud voice.

"It's simply a case of replacing the wire, Eva," Millwood said. "You can do that, I'm sure."

"Of course, Captain. It won't take long."

He climbed down the ladder. "Crane, stand by to assist Officer Zachrisson."

"Aye, aye, sir."

"Everything's crystal clear now!" Millwood exclaimed. "The bared wire shorted out the feedback signal that should have stopped the servo motor moving the bow planes. So the motor kept on tilting the planes upward and we kept on pointing toward the ice canopy at an ever-increasing angle." God! It had been a lucky thing he'd reacted fast enough to order manual control and pivot the planes downward. Otherwise— He shuddered.

"That's it," Eva said, with a note of finality. She snapped shut the cover of the distribution box and climbed down.

"Ready to test?" Millwood asked.

"Aye, aye, Captain."

She crossed to her console and checked the switches. Her finger poised over a button, then she pressed it. A signal light lit up, indicating that the automatic sonar system controlling the bow planes was operational.

"Good. Very good," Millwood said. He took his hand off the diving lever and watched the depth gauge. "She's responding normally on automatic," he announced with satisfaction. "Now, if we could only stop the lousy leak."

He checked *North Star*'s position and saw with relief that they were well clear of Lancaster Sound and off Baffin Island. Now that he was hugging the coast on the southward leg an ice-free sea couldn't be far away. He hoped they didn't run afoul of the Baffin Bay ice pack that *Nautilus*'s commander had told him about: a huge ice island that floated up and down the Bay at the whim of currents and winds. Estimated to measure fifteen miles by six, with sheer cliffs sixty feet high, the massive floating island was reported to have wide bays and indentations from which hundreds of icebergs broke off and drifted south. He remembered one almanac reporting several islands of this size drifting between Greenland and Baffin Island. But now time was all-important. He'd already run an oil slick through part of the Passage. He must avoid, by any means left to him, spilling oil through Davis Strait, where it could drift south into the Labrador Sea.

This time he was going to play it safe and, if possible, avoid coming up through thick ice. He glanced at the monitoring screens. They were getting lighter despite the swirls of oil picked up by the camera.

"Harding, cut power to zero. We're going to surface."

"Aye, aye, Captain."

He waited for the vessel to slow. At last he said, "Stand by to surface, Harding."

"Aye, aye, Captain."

"Eva! Keep a sharp lookout on the sonarscopes. There may be icebergs as we come up."

85

"Yes, Captain."

"First notch on the ballast tanks."

"Aye, aye, Captain."

The depth gauge slowly unwound. The pinging grew louder.

"Monitoring screens, Eva?"

"Light gray. Oil."

Ninety feet . . . 80 . . . 70. She was rising steadily on an even keel and it was going to be all right. Fifty . . . 40 . . . 30.

A see-saw action rocked the control room. Probably the effects of a surface swell as the sail reached the upper layers; a good sign. It meant no ice. He'd be able to radio their position in a few minutes. The depth gauge turned more slowly now. He felt *North Star* rolling and heard the gurgle of water.

"Surfaced!" he called, aware of the relief in his voice. The sea slopped against the hull.

"Eva, switch on surface radar." He waited for the screen before him to light up and stabilize. In a moment a finger of light started its steady wheeling motion as the scope filled with a pale green translucence. At the center a bright dot indicated *North Star*'s position. Several hazy formless shapes emerged behind the tracing radius of the finger. He peered closer, puzzled.

"They look like spurious reflections or radar ghosts to me, Harding. What do you make of them?"

Harding shrugged. "There's a bit of scatter too, Captain. Probably off wave crests. It's a murky picture. Doesn't show much."

"Up periscope, Harding. We'll see what's going on out there."

He clamped his eyes to the glass. "Funny. Not a goddamned thing," he said. "The oil must have clouded the lens."

"Why was it clear the last time we surfaced, Captain?" Eva asked. It was a logical question, and he didn't know how to reply, so he said nothing. Instead, he swung the scope around and adjusted the focusing control. The glass was opaque in every direction.

"Follow me, Harding!" He climbed the ladder, hesitated before the panel on the bridge, then pushed the button. The hatch slid open and clouds of steam billowed into the sail, driven before a strong breeze. He was conscious of the moist smell of a thick sea fog.

On the platform the damp air seeped through his jacket and clung to his shirt. The wind swirled the fog around the steps. It was queer seeing fog blown before the wind; it usually hugged the water surface as a warm front came up across cold water. But this was the Artic, he reminded himself, where anything could happen. The fog was so thick he couldn't see the bow.

"If the oil level in the tanks is below the rupture, then at least the damned oil has quit leaking Harding," he said. "The hole must be out of the water now."

Eva moved behind him, and Simoncelli exclaimed, "A real pea-souper!"

"It gets right into your bones," Eva said, shivering. Millwood took a step down to the deck, grasping the rail, straining to see forward. The mist suddenly cleared and for a fleeting moment he saw *North Star*'s bow—then it vanished. But instead of the fog swirling back to fill the void, a huge white cliff thrust itself through the moist blanket, towering above him. There was a shattering roar as the mountain toppled toward him and fell across the deck.

"Back!" he yelled. He hurled himself through the hatch and landed on Simoncelli's belly. The floor shuddered and tilted toward the bow. A staccato drumming of heavy blows, like a jackhammer being driven through the hull, filled the air.

He heard Eva call out as she crouched on the floor near the ladder to the control room, clinging to the handrail. When the crashing sounds subsided he shouted, "It's all right! Sounds worse than it really is!"

"An iceberg! It was right on top of us!" Harding yelled. At that moment Crane's head appeared at the top of the ladder, his usually placid face looking worried.

Millwood scrambled to the hatch and looked out. The fog had completely closed in, reducing visibility to twenty feet. Slabs of ice on the deck slid fore and aft as the vessel pitched. The berg had left massive ice boulders on the foredeck, weighing *North Star* down. He worried about another berg out there in the fog. At least their forward motion was stopped now, and they were drifting in the same current as the ice. Further collisions were unlikely. Better get a radio message off right away. Suddenly a white glow appeared above them. The fog was lifting. The mist on deck receded, exposing the bow.

"My God!" he groaned.

"Jesus! The bow's been mangled!" Simoncelli cried. "The oil's gushing out like a wildcatter!"

"Harding! Get lifelines! We're going to inspect the damage."

Harding picked up two coils of rope.

"Crane! Secure the ends around the platform rail. Help lash me in." He swung the end of the rope around his shoulders and under his armpits. Crane quickly lashed a rope around Harding in a similar manner.

"Crane. Stand on the platform and pay out the lines as Harding and I go for'ard."

"Aye, aye, sir!"

Millwood stepped onto the platform, just as the fog whirled in again, enclosing him in a white damp blanket. He waited for the breeze to blow away until the bow was again exposed.

"Watch the ice on deck, Harding. Keep close."

He heard Eva's voice, distorted by the fog. "Be careful, Frank!" An ice boulder barred his way. "Follow me," he shouted, stepping carefully around it. A sudden breeze swept the deck clear, and he groped his way forward, checking that his second-in-command had negotiated the ice safely. The deck was already sloping down at the bow and he felt *North Star* wallowing. At the round-down he stopped, staring at the mixture of oil and sea water spreading across the sea. He looked up and peered ahead, but the fog limited visibility to fifty feet beyond the vessel's bow.

"Secure my lifeline! I'm going over the round-down."

"Take it easy, Captain."

He felt the frigid steel under his hands. Everything had happened so quickly he'd had no time to think about putting on a parka or gloves. A thick ice floe slithered along the deck and for one dreadful moment he thought it would smash into him, but *North Star* dipped and the ice flew into the sea, drenching his trousers with oily scum. Slowly he lowered himself over the side, feet balancing against the vessel's plates. Another five feet and he came in line with the buckled plates and exposed stringers, twisted like pieces of spaghetti. Lowering himself another two feet he found himself looking into a cavernous opening, partially choked with blocks of ice where the berg had struck, big enough to drive a truck through. Every time *North Star* lifted to the sea a great wave of black crude oil gushed out of the cavern and poured out to the accompaniment of loud gurgling sounds as water rushed in to replace the oil. There was no way they could plug a hole that size. Even as he hung poised over the opening a wave rolled into the hole and, as the vessel pitched, oil streamed out. His stomach retched with the fumes.

"Haul up, Harding!"

After he'd clambered on deck he looked at Harding for a long moment before replying to the question in the other's eye. He shook his head. "There's no way we can plug her. She's going."

Harding stared at him incredulously, muscles on his face working.

"We may be able to stay aboard an hour—two if we're very lucky. It'll give us time to radio Boston."

The fog suddenly engulfed them. He tugged on the lifeline and yelled, "Crane! Haul in!"

He felt the line grow taut and followed it across the deck with Harding, making detours around the ice blocks.

"Well, sir?" Crane said, when they stepped inside the sail.

"Listen, everybody," he said, looking around at the quartet of strained faces. "The berg made a hole that's too big to plug." He turned to Simoncelli. "The oil's coming out too fast, Oscar. We can't stop it."

Simoncelli looked unbelievingly at Millwood. "Jesus Christ! All this way . . ."

"We're sinking, Captain?" Eva's voice was almost inaudible.

He nodded. "Yes," he said, but the sound of the seas breaking against the bows and the screeching of ice as it slid off the sloping deck drowned out his voice.

"Harding, get the rubber raft on the floor at standby," he shouted.

"How long have we got, sir?" Crane called.

"About an hour—maybe two. If the weather deteriorates the seas will work their way deeper into the hull and replace the oil quicker, of course. The oil's bound to give her some buoyancy, but we can't depend on that. We must radio Boston."

Eva made a step toward the ladder.

"Stay up here, Eva. I'll make the call. Make Mr. Simoncelli as comfortable as you can."

"I'm comfortable as I am," Simoncelli snapped indignantly.

Millwood looked at him. "With an arm like that you need as much comfort as you can get. You stay up here. That's an order," he added.

In the control room the forward tilt seemed more pronounced.

"Harding. Up antenna. If we can't get Boston try that guy at Baker Lake."

He turned to Crane. "Raise the control rods in the nuclear reactor to stop the chain reaction. Otherwise when she goes she'll make the seabed radioactive. One type of pollution's enough," he said grimly.

"Aye, aye, sir." Crane crossed to the power control panel, worked the switches, and checked the response of the reactor. In the background Millwood heard Harding speaking into the radiophone.

Harding looked up. "Boston's dead, Captain!"

"Don't waste time. Get on to that Baker Lake guy. His waveband's in Eva's book."

Harding found the band and switched wave bands. "Submarine tanker *North Star* calling Baker Lake. Come in." His second-in-command's face was strained under the lights. He repeated the call several times. At last he turned to Millwood. "He doesn't answer, Captain."

"Try him once more."

He waited as Harding tried again. There was no answer. Suddenly the floor lurched.

Simoncelli bellowed from the sail, "You'd better get up

here! She's tilting like a falling oil rig!"

"Harding—Crane—up to the sail. Get everybody into parkas. It's going to be cold on the water!"

"What about you, Captain?" Harding said.

"I'll send a Mayday signal. I'll follow you in a second. Get moving!"

He waited to make sure they climbed the ladder, crossed to the radio panel, and switched on the emergency radio.

"Mayday! Mayday! Mayday! Submarine tanker *North Star* has collided with an iceberg and is sinking at latitude sixty-seven degrees, forty-eight point two minutes north; longitude sixty-three degrees, thirty minutes west. Mayday . . ." As he gave the figures his mind considered the irony of a submarine colliding with an iceberg on the surface. All the scientific devices and failsafe systems and the forward and upward scanning sonar and radar, and a goddamned berg crashes down on him while he's nearly stationary on the surface!

"For God's sake, Frank! Get up here!" Simoncelli's voice roared down the companionway. Millwood repeated the message into the microphone, switched off, and ran along the corridor to his cabin. He searched frantically among the books on the shelf as the floor slope increased. Where the hell was it? *Arctic Pilot.* His eyes skimmed the titles. There! Savagely he yanked out the leatherbound book and ran through the door.

He darted into the control room, grabbed the vessel's logbook, and glanced at the cargo gauges, with their rapidly dropping needles. Simoncelli thundered, insistently, "Frank, get going!"

"Coming!" he called. For a moment he stood at the bottom of the ladder and looked around the control room. The lights on Eva's console flashed dire warnings of red and comforting messages of green. Then he climbed up into the sail and peered through the hatch. The fog had lifted. A pool of crude oil had spread wide over the surface of the sea, glinting where it caught the pale light, and the bow was awash. About a hundred yards away, surrounded by ice cakes, was the rest of the berg that had crashed down on them, a mountain of ice more than two hundred feet high. It sailed along with a malignant aloofness. He focused on the rubberized fabric package the others had maneuvered onto the floor. As he did so he saw a gold button. Instinctively he bent down, picked it up and slipped it into his jacket pocket.

"Harding! Grab that clip on the end of the safety lanyard as soon as we get the raft through the hatch!"

"Aye, aye, Captain!"

Everybody was in a parka. He motioned to the rack behind him. "Take some of the oilskins." He was conscious of the frigid air in the sail as he pulled on his own parka.

"Eva first, then you, Oscar, then Crane and Harding. I'll bring up the rear. Now!"

Eva stepped onto the platform. She hesitated on the top of the three steps that led down to the deck. Crude oil was already licking the foredeck less than a hundred feet away.

"Get moving!" Millwood shouted.

She stepped to the deck, gripping the rail at the platform's base, Simoncelli moved out, then Crane, supporting the end of the inflatable raft. Harding and Millwood followed, taking the weight. In a few seconds the raft lay on the deck. Harding handed the clip to Millwood. He checked that the lanyard was free, opened the jaws of the clip around the rail, and tested it for security. Bending down, he gave the lanyard a steady pull, and instantly there was a hissing sound as the compressed air bottles inside the package inflated the raft.

"Grab it!" he shouted as the unfolding raft moved. "Don't let it get away!"

"It doesn't look very solid," Simoncelli said, surveying the ten-foot-round craft, on which a weather hood had automatically popped up.

Millwood looked at the sky. Directly overhead were thin clouds with underlying wisps scudding by, indicating deteriorating weather. The oil, already spread a hundred yards to port and starboard of the vessel's bow, now lapped amidships.

"Everybody lift. We'll launch it from the stern to clear the oil. Harding, pay out the lanyard as we go."

The raft seemed lighter inflated. When they had it on the stern deck, Millwood looked down. *North Star* was already so far down at the bow that the stern deck had risen ten feet higher out of the water than normal. He couldn't delay now.

"Eva! Get aboard!"

She looked hesitantly at the raft. "It's all right," he assured her. "We'll launch it with you aboard." She lifted the flap and stepped inside.

"Now, Harding—Crane! gently down the side!" He felt the heavy rubber material give as he pushed. "Steady!"

The raft plopped into the water at an angle. It quickly rode high and level. "Now you, Oscar," he said, casting an anxious glance at the oil sweeping aft along *North Star*'s sides. He gripped the old man's shoulder and, with the other hand, pulled the lanyard tight to keep the raft alongside the vessel. Simoncelli crouched and lowered himself into the raft. Eva extended her hand, and he stepped aboard.

"Now you, Crane." He tightened his hold on the lanyard as his engineering officer slithered down the rounded side and into the raft.

"Get aboard, Harding!"

His second-in-command skillfully slipped over the side and into the bobbing raft.

RAGE UNDER THE ARCTIC

Millwood gave one final look around the deck, slid down the side, and climbed in. Releasing another clip securing the opposite end of the lanyard to the raft, he threw it overboard. It clanged metallically against *North Star*'s side like a death knell.

"Quick! The paddle!"

He rammed it against the submarine and pushed. A narrow arm of sea surged between the raft and the vessel, and the gap widened. A couple of dozen hard strokes and they were ten yards clear. He was aware of the others' silence as they peered through the flap of the raft at *North Star*, dipping deeper at the bow as the oily swell gripped her. His stroking became less frantic as the agony of leaving the sinking submarine suddenly swept over him.

"Eva, get out the radio beacon in that rubber pocket," he said. "And there's a hand compass in the next pocket and a sextant."

"What about grub?" Simoncelli said, a worried look on his face.

"Your belly again!" Millwood managed to force a grin. "Emergency rations are over there," he said, pointing to another pocket, "but they are to be left strictly alone for the present. Eva, get the beacon operating. Somebody'll pick up the signal."

"Here's the compass, Captain," said Eva, handing him a small instrument. He stuffed it carefully under his parka into the pocket of his jacket. Eva removed the radio beacon from its container.

"The antenna sticks through that hole in the hood. Take out the plug," he directed.

She pulled out the telescoping rod, removed the little rubber plug in the canopy and pushed the antenna through. When she turned a small knob an orange lamp pulsated, indicating

95

automatic transmission of their distress signal.

Across fifty yards of water now, *North Star* still floated stern high. Oil and water sloshed over the base of the sail. He wondered how long it would be before the water rose as far as the hatch and poured into the sail, already wallowing with the action of the heavy swell.

"Is this all we do, just sit and wait?" Simoncelli said irritably.

"Buck up, Oscar. It won't be long before someone comes. That beacon's got a hundred-mile range, more if the weather permits. And land's only about ten miles away. Look, you can see it from here."

"Where? Let me see!" Simoncelli demanded. He stood unsteadily behind Millwood, peering at the line of land to the west. "Well, thank God for that!" he said in a more cheerful voice.

"It looks closer than ten miles," Eva added.

Millwood looked anxiously at the darkening northern horizon, where an odd streak of aurora flickered behind the clouds. Another storm was brewing in the north, and the easterly wind would blow it toward shore. He'd expected to see signs of the recent storm in Lancaster Sound still visible in the west. He moved the raft around and inspected the eastern sky. Thick black stratus clouds rimmed the horizon. Paddling the raft around so that the opening faced south, he saw the same ominous build-up there.

"Doesn't look promising," Crane said soberly.

Millwood shrugged. "Can't tell what it'll do. It's chancy in these waters. Storms and blizzards come up quickly, even in summer." To divert attention from the weather, he pointed to *North Star*. "She's taking her time sinking!"

He knelt at the opening, the others behind him, balancing their bodies against the bobbing of the raft, watching *North*

Star, now completely encircled by oil. Her bow had swung into the swell, but the deck and sail were still above water.

"She's *not* sinking!" Eva cried.

"It must be the oil," Millwood replied. "It's helping to keep her afloat."

His vision of a huge oil spill spreading across the open waters and the ice fields receded. If help came soon they might be able to board and salvage *North Star,* patch her up, and have her towed in. He glanced at the radio beacon to check that it was still transmitting its coded distress message. The orange light blinked back reassuringly. He scanned the sea and the sky, from horizon to horizon. Nothing. He pulled the *Arctic Pilot* out of his pocket and flipped the pages until he found the description of the east coast of Baffin Island.

"What are you looking for?" Simoncelli said.

"Trying to fix our position." There was a small-scale map in the *Pilot.* With his finger he traced *North Star's* passage where he'd hugged the coast a few miles off the ice field to shorten the route south. He turned the pages quickly. Cape Mercy, Hoare Bay, Cape Dyer. The description wasn't cheering: high cliffs rising directly from the sea, steep indented rocky coastline. Nothing favorable for a landing.

He measured the distance on the little map. The beacon's signal might be picked up at Cape Dyer. In any case, they were drifting south, caught in the massive tidal flow that quickened and became the swifter Labrador Current.

"We're here." He held up the map for the others to see. "Opposite Broughton Island, north of Cape Dyer." He added cheerfully, "There's a Dewline base at Cape Dyer called Dye Main."

He looked again at the distant coast, following the contour from the mountains in the background to the thin blue ribbon at the waterline. That would be the ice field, extending out to sea. He consulted the *Pilot* and read aloud: " 'Deep glaciated valleys and steep corries have cut indentations in the coast. Small irregular inlets . . . depths over eighty fathoms . . . ice fields extend for some considerable distance from the shore, even in summer.' " He lapsed into silence and read the rest to himself: "Strong tidal rips in shoal areas have been observed near the coast on the few occasions when the ice has broken up. Winds rise quickly and blow strongly along the axis of the bay owing to the channeling effect of the high shores."

"Well?" Simoncelli demanded.

"Just more of the same," he said, shoving the book into his pocket.

"Doesn't sound healthy to me," Simoncelli asserted.

"What about a bite to eat?" suggested Millwood.

"I want your opinion on our chances first," said Simoncelli.

Millwood looked at the old man sitting uncomfortably on the wooden lattice seat opposite, his right arm dangling awkwardly in its sling, the parka hood thrown back over his shoulders. Simoncelli was wearing a defiant expression. He was clearly at the end of his reserve and wouldn't be put off.

"All right, Oscar. I'll give it to you straight. Unless some patrolling aircraft picks up our beacon, we'll have to sit it out until we drift south within range of Cape Dyer. It's about a hundred and thirty miles away."

Nobody spoke, so he continued. "The alternative is to take turns with the paddle and try to make it to the coast." He nodded toward the west. "But there's an ice field that may extend five or more miles out to sea. You can see it from here —that bluish-white line. We'd have to leave the relative safety of the raft and walk across the ice field. It's terribly risky."

"Like falling through a crevasse in the ice?" Harding suggested.

"Yes. None of us has any experience in crossing ice fields."
He stopped abruptly, remembering Simoncelli's Yukon days.

"I crossed an ice field in northern Canada on ——"

"When you were young," Millwood interrupted, "and with
two good arms. Oscar, let's face facts. You're in no condition
to tramp miles across the ice. And I don't fancy it, and I'm
sure Eva doesn't. We'll stay where we are, drift with the
current, and wait until somebody picks up our beacon. In the
meantime, let's have some chow!"

Eva broke the seal of the airtight package and pulled out
several plastic containers. Inside were toothpaste-tube-like
containers and sealed bottles of large capsules. Millwood was
reminded of televised pictures of astronauts eating on their
way to the moon. Eva handed Simoncelli a tube. "It's con-
centrated protein. Sorry it doesn't come in three flavors!"

"Jesus Christ! Is that the best they can do?" the old man
grumbled.

"There's also vitamin C—keeps away scurvy—and some
chocolate," said Eva cheerfully.

"All we need now is a toddy of rum, and it'll be like old
times," Millwood added quietly.

"You mean you've been wrecked like this before, Captain?"
asked Eva incredulously.

He was about to open his mouth to reply when a plane
swooshed overhead.

"He's coming back!" Millwood yelled, watching the four-
engined turboprop bank and turn.

The plane came toward them, low over the sea, its engines
throttled back. "It's an antisub reconnaissance aircraft," he
said, recognizing the outline of a Lockheed P-3B. It had approached from the south—no wonder they hadn't heard it—
and was probably on its way back to base at Thule, Greenland. As it flew by less than a hundred feet away, he saw the

copilot wave and give the thumbs-up sign. Then it was past and out of sight, hidden by the raft's hood. Millwood thrust the paddle into the sea and swiveled the craft. The airplane turned away, readying for another pass, but this time it flew over *North Star*, now almost invisible below the wave crests. He heard the distant sound of a marker buoy whistling down, saw its parachute open, and imagined the activity on board: the radio operator flashing a message reporting their position and *North Star*'s, and the activity at Thule, or perhaps Dye Main, signaling a helicopter or vessel to come to pick them up.

The plane made one more pass over them, dipped its wings, and headed northeast. As its sound died away he was conscious of the slap of the sea against the sides of the raft. It had happened so quickly that now he felt deserted.

"How long before they send help?" Eva said.

"Not long, now they know our position," he replied. "It all depends where they send help from, Thule or Cape Dyer. There may even be—hey, listen!"

He poked his head out of the opening. The sky was empty, but he heard the distinct *flump-flump-flump* of helicopter rotor blades approaching.

"Where the hell's the paddle!" he shouted, groping around until he found it and thrust it into the water. "There he is." He pointed at a helicopter coming in low from the south.

"What a beautiful sight!" exclaimed Simoncelli.

Millwood watched the small helicopter approach. It was equipped with pontoons, with the numerals 801 painted in white on the fuselage. As it circled the raft, he could see only one person aboard, the pilot, staring down at them. The sound of the engine slackened and the rotor blades slowed. It hovered momentarily over the wave tops and came gently to rest on the water less than fifty yards downwind of the raft.

Millwood paddled vigorously, maneuvering the raft sideways, aiming it at the middle of the starboard pontoon. A door in the side opened and a pink-cheeked face appeared. The pilot looked no more than a boy. A rope curled down. "Catch!" he shouted.

SIX

From the air *North Star* was a slender gray shape surrounded by a huge disc of black oil. Long fingerlike slicks had broken from the circle and were drifting separately in a southerly direction, giving the dull sea an opaque sheen.

"You guys are lucky! I mean lucky, sir, Captain," the pilot said, looking embarrassed. "Pilot Kelly, sir. United States Air Force." He couldn't have been much more than twenty, Millwood thought, just out of helicopter training school. "Normally never get this far north but I was on special patrol from Cape Dyer. Got the signal from the antisub aircraft out of Thule that he'd spotted you. I'd just been recalled. There's a helluva storm building up over Dyer. I don't know if we can make it back there now. Half a second, Captain."

Kelly adjusted his headset and pushed a button. "Helicopter eight-zero-one to Dye Main," he said. "Have taken aboard the crew of submarine *North Star*. The vessel is afloat and leaking oil at. . . ." He read off the position from his chart. "Request met report on weather at base."

He pressed the headphones close to his ears to hear above

the roar of the engine. Millwood saw color drain from the rosy cheeks. "You're socked in completely down there?" Kelly's eyes narrowed in concentration. "How long before all the coast's socked in?" He stared ahead under blond eyebrows. The rocky coast was now clearly visible, the distant ice field glinting under the midday light. Kelly leaned forward and switched off the radio. "Dye Main's socked in with a full blizzard and we've been diverted up the coast. 'Find any Eskimo village where there's a landing spot,' they said. Fast as we can!"

"We're going back up the coast? The way we came in *North Star?*" Millwood said.

Kelly nodded and peered ahead anxiously. "Pity this little buggy doesn't have the range to make Thule." He worked the controls and the machine swung around until it faced the northwest. It gathered speed. Millwood looked at the altimeter. Five hundred feet.

"Dye Main knows about the wreck?" he said.

"We've known all along about your troubles, sir."

"Boston told you?"

"Yes, sir. It's been in all the newspapers. Now Dye Main knows *North Star*'s position, they'll order the salvage fleet out."

"Salvage fleet?" A mixture of relief and self-blame passed through Millwood.

"It's been assembling for days down south. Ready to help when you surfaced, sir. And there're oil clean-up experts." He looked at the sky, his face contorted with worry.

"Where're you making for, Kelly?"

"This Eskimo village up the coast, here." He put his finger on the chart.

"Kivitooluk?"

Kelly nodded. "I've been there once before. It's sheltered by an inlet and some high cliffs. About a hundred and fifty miles north'norwest of Dye Main."

"How's your gas?" Millwood said, and then regretted asking. The kid knows his job, don't hurt his feelings, he reminded himself.

Kelly glanced at the instrument panel. "We're okay, sir. Plenty."

"How long will it take to get there?"

Kelly checked the chart and glanced at his watch. "About an hour and twenty minutes, sir. Hope it's not socked in too. There was a bad blizzard up this whole east coast a few days ago. The worst in living memory. A number of Eskimo settlements have been cut off for days. Haven't been able to make contact."

"Is Kivitooluk a small village?"

"A big settlement as Eskimo villages go, sir. About two hundred Eskimos and a dozen Canadians from down south. There's a weather station and a trading post." Kelly switched on the radio. "I'll tell them we're coming," he said, forcing a grin.

"Calling weather station Kivitooluk. Helicopter eight-zero-one diverted from Dye Main," he said into the microphone. "We expect to arrive at Kivitooluk in about one hour twenty minutes. Over."

Millwood watched as Kelly again pressed the headphones close. A tuft of fair hair poked from behind his ear. He heard Kelly repeat the message.

"Can't understand it, sir," he said, pressing another switch. He scratched his head. "Looks like they're all out on strike or something. They're not answering."

Millwood shrugged. "Try them again in a few minutes. Maybe it's just a temporary radio blackout. It happens sometimes in the Arctic." Again he regretted telling the young pilot how to do his job.

The ice field was coming up diagonally on the port quarter. He saw that the ice, which from the raft had appeared to be a blue glint on the horizon, actually was a dull gray color. As they sped toward it his heart sank. A familiar dark stain covered the water at the edge of the ice. He saw the slicks snaking along, parallel to the ice. If the oil that had leaked from *North Star* on their run down this part of the coast already had reached the edge of the ice field, what about the bulk of the cargo still in *North Star*'s hull? There'd be one hell of a spill if it all escaped: the biggest in maritime history.

In a few minutes they were over the oil, running in close to the ice field. It must have been leaking faster than he'd estimated. Oil was everywhere. Then they were directly over the ice, where the current opened a wide channel. Black floes floated like burned pancakes in a sea of brownish fat. The action of the waves rolling in from the open sea, combined with high winds, had sprayed the oil upward, scattering it far and wide over the ice field. Millwood stared down, filled with dismay.

"Look over there!" Eva cried, pointing.

Millwood stared at the big sluglike shapes lying ahead. There were hundreds of them covering the ice, shiny black forms lying in groups of twos and threes.

"Let's go take a look," Kelly said, twisting the controls. The helicopter hovered a hundred feet over the nearest forms. They were motionless.

"Harp seals," Kelly said. "They come south this time of year to breed."

Millwood gasped. He stared at the carcasses. The pairs nearly all consisted of one large seal and a smaller one cuddled against it. "Pups, too."

Kelly nodded. He pulled the helicopter to three hundred feet and moved it forward, slower now. Millwood looked ahead at the rugged snow-capped mountains. At their feet was a wide coastal plain, a brown line in the distance. He questioned Kelly. "Why didn't they take to the land?"

"Harp seals never go ashore, sir."

"You mean they just stayed there and let the oil smother them?"

Kelly shrugged. Millwood got the impression he wasn't greatly concerned, but then, he wasn't responsible. What must it be like farther north where *North Star* had left a trail across the Arctic? With anguish he thought of the huge herds of seals in the Northwest Passage, and polar bears.

"The oil must have sealed their breathing holes, sir," Kelly said. "Look there!"

In a narrow lead in the ice was a small whale, which Millwood instantly identified as a beluga. Rather than its natural dazzling white, it was a slimy black, floating head down with its humped back raised clear of the gummy water. Not far away in another channel were two others, also humped and head down, the flukes of one frozen to the surface of the brownish ice when the whale had flipped over one last time in its struggle to escape the choking scum and oily fumes. He remembered Simoncelli's delight when they had sighted belugas only a few days before. The scene of the plunging carefree creatures flashed through his mind.

He spotted a movement between hummocks of ice about a quarter mile away. "Over there," he instructed, and Kelly slewed the helicopter, hovering above outcrops of partly clear ice at the center of a large floe. Except for the island of white, the floe was covered with wind-blown oil.

"Walruses," Millwood said, seeing blobs with tusks. "They're alive?"

"Just barely," Kelly said. Millwood stared at the four splotched animals. As the helicopter dropped lower, the biggest animal drew back on its flippers in a defiant attitude, glaring upward, its bristly muzzle working angrily. It was a bull defending three cows, and they were probably all that remained of the harem the bull had managed to drive on to the ice before the oil smothered the others.

"They might make it to shore when the ice shifts," he said, surveying the crazed pattern of the ice field. It had broken into large floes separated by leads as the storm had abated and the inexorable southern ocean drift had resumed. Kelly raised his shoulders in a helpless gesture, then turned the controls, and they moved off in the direction of the land, passing over the blackened coastal ice field in silence. Millwood saw a high promontory rising sheer out of the water ahead. Kelly consulted the chart.

"There's an inlet past that rock," he said. "I remember now, sir."

"Try Kivitooluk again, Kelly," Millwood said.

Kelly flipped a switch. "Dye Main helicopter eight-zero-one calling Kivitooluk weather station. Over!"

Millwood saw Kelly's lips tighten. He called again, "Dye Main helicopter eight-zero-one calling Kivitooluk. Over!" He turned and looked at Millwood, who recognized the suppressed fear that clutched at his own gut. Kelly twisted the knobs on the radio panel. "Damned crazy guys, why don't you answer?" He turned to Millwood again. "It's absolutely dead. Not even static or background noise."

"Perhaps they had to close down the station on account of the blizzard, or the wind could have knocked their antenna down." Millwood could tell that his explanation hadn't convinced anyone. Kelly leaned forward and flipped off the switch.

The breaks in the ice were more frequent now, and the oily seas clearly visible, irridescent where the light caught them. Millwood saw the sea break against the jagged windward edges of the ice, throwing brown spume over the surface of the floes. During the blizzard the spray must have been picked up by the wind and driven horizontally across the ice in an airborne storm of emulsified droplets. That had happened in Chedabucto Bay, Nova Scotia, when a gale whipped up oil off the surface of the sea after the tanker *Arrow* had been wrecked. Houses set well back from the beach in a fishing village had been spattered with a tarry substance that had driven people from their homes. Parked cars had been plastered with oil and had to be steam-cleaned before they could be used again.

A craggy headland with snow on the top loomed ahead. Kelly turned the helicopter in from the ice field and pointed. "Up the inlet, turn right into the bay, and Kivitooluk's at the top." He positioned the craft to proceed up the center of the inlet, warning his passengers to hold tight, and expect downdrafts from the hills.

Ahead lay the dark edge of the ice with the rolling sea breaking against it. The helicopter swung to the right, and Millwood looked into a bay flanked by bleak cliffs, their edges starkly outlined. Directly ahead he could make out a low beach, the path of a frozen, snow-covered river and its shallow delta where, during high summer, it emptied into the bay. Set well back on the beach was a collection of houses. There were about forty grubby-looking buildings scattered along a narrow road, and a trail led down to the beach. In the middle of the settlement was a large building, with a reddish roof, and farther back, at the foot of the hills, was another, larger structure, with a tall antenna close by. "The antenna's still standing," he said, feeling his stomach tighten.

RAGE UNDER THE ARCTIC

"Look!" Simoncelli shouted, making a stabbing downward gesture with his thumb.

They were coming in over the beach where an oil-slicked lagoon lay directly beneath the helicopter. A smashed kayak floated in the middle of it, a harpoon and rope in a tangled mess on the foredeck. The derelict craft was awash with emulsified liquid, rising and falling with the suck of the tide. A curve of dark water lapped against the pebbled beach, and rainbow eddies swirled away. In the crescent lay thick blobs. Millwood saw that the shapes were the bodies of seabirds.

"Eskimo curlews, by their size," Kelly commented.

A silvery line farther along the beach caught Millwood's attention. "Kelly, over there."

"Yes, sir."

"Jesus Christ," said Simoncelli. Thousands of fish lay belly up on the frozen shore. Waves broke with scummy crests rising and falling on the fish, washing them higher up the pebbled beach. There was no sign of life anywhere in all the dismal scene. Millwood's whole being ached to be away from the place.

"Where the hell is everybody?" Kelly said.

Kelly settled the machine on the beach. Nobody spoke as the rotor slowed and stopped. Millwood stared ahead, up the narrow oil-slicked road, hoping somebody would come out of the wooden shacks to greet them. For a full minute he sat glued to his seat, waiting. At last he opened the door and glanced up at the leaden sky.

"Try the radio now, Kelly," he said, his hand on the door handle.

Kelly switched on. "Helicopter eight-zero-one calling Kivitooluk weather station. Over."

Millwood could feel the silence. Kelly shook his head.

"Try Dye Main."

Kelly turned a knob. "Helicopter eight-zero-one calling Dye Main. Have landed at Kivitooluk. There's no sign of life here. Over."

Millwood heard a thin scream from the earphones on Kelly's head. Kelly pulled them away. "I can hear a voice but not a word of what he's saying, sir."

"Try again. Must be the storm."

"Helicopter eight-zero-one to Dye Main. Have landed at Kivitooluk. Nobody here!" Again Millwood heard the earphones scream shrilly. Kelly turned to him. "It's so distorted I can't make it out. Here, see if you can understand, sir."

Millwood took the headphones. He winced as he listened to the completely unintelligible, high-pitched voice, and handed the headpiece back. "Atmospherics," he said. "That's that for a while. Now, let's see what's doing here. At least we can get out of the weather."

He lowered himself to the ground and felt his boots slip. "Take it easy," he warned. "The muck's made it slippery."

They drove spikes deep into the ground and lashed the helicopter to them. A light snow started to fall, but within a few minutes it suddenly cleared and for a brief spell a watery sun shone through a gap in the clouds. Millwood led them up the beach, still hoping to see someone run out to greet them, but he knew it would not happen. He moved toward the first house. The roof had been ripped off. "Some blizzard," Kelly said, scooping a handful of crusted snow from the side of the house. He held it out for Millwood to inspect. "Look, sir, it's like rice pudding with too many raisins."

Millwood examined the snow. It was hard and lumpy, with droplets of oil embedded in tiny crystals of ice. The droplets must have been caught in midair and enveloped with spray as the seas crashed on the edge of the ice field. The gale would do the rest, gathering them up and flinging them like hail into the village.

"What's that?" Crane asked. He indicated a mound of stones some distance away. Millwood walked ahead, stumbling over the greasy ground. The cracks were filled with jellied oil. "It's some form of storage," he said.

"It's where they kept their fish, sir," Kelly said. "A cache."

"Get them out from the top, eh?"

"I guess so, sir."

Millwood climbed up the mound, his feet slithering in the oily snow. The top had been ripped open and the stones hurled aside. As he peered down into the hollow, he was over-powered by a foul smell of fish and oil.

"Ugh!" he said, dropping to the ground. "They must have tried to save the fish and then been forced to leave."

He looked at the deserted house. A sled was wedged at the bottom of the seaward-facing wall. The door swung open in the breeze, and he looked inside. It was a one-room house, now open to the sky. The walls inside were completely spattered with tar. A small window in the land-facing wall that had once let in some light was now stained with scum.

There was a table in the middle of the room, with an open can of greasy beans on it. A sodden bed rested against the far wall. A pair of snowshoes lay on the floor. He tried to close the door, but it was jammed.

He rejoined the others. Except for the breeze that soughed through the broken boards of the houses, it was deathly silent. He tried to visualize the scene: the darkening sky, the first rush of the wind, Eskimo wives hurrying from the trading post, dragging tightly bundled kids, turning up the oil stoves a notch as soon as they got home. There must have been anxious glances seaward for husbands out on the ice, hunting seals, and the sealers watching the sea and sky and knowing when to break off and make for the safety of land. Then there had been a long, dark night of horror in the wooden houses: the sound of windows smashing in the gale, the tearing screech of roofs peeling off, the rush to help neighbors and the sudden surprise as they fell on the slimy road; the congealed globules of half-frozen oil, stinging their faces, making breathing difficult, smearing eyes and fur-trimmed parkas. He shivered and turned to the others.

Then suddenly he heard a low moan. For a moment he thought it might be the wind freshening, but then the sound rose to a spine-chilling cry, echoing eerily between the buildings and the distant crags.

He was conscious of the vapor of his breath billowing before his eyes. The cry was half human, half animal. It trailed off in a shrill wail and died to a final, heartbreaking whimper. He looked at the others. They were frozen with fear, staring toward the village.

"Come on!" he shouted, turning up the road. The others followed hesitantly, treading carefully. A hundred yards before the red-roofed building, he stopped. Across the top of it he made out the partly obliterated sign: HUDSON'S BAY COMPANY and, in smaller letters below, TRADING POST. The others gathered around, huddling close to him. Only the wind whined through the settlement. He could feel the sweat chill his back as the breeze tugged at his parka.

As he moved toward the trading post, it came again, louder now. First the moan, then the cry, plaintive and hollow, filled with desolation and despair, falling away thinly into a final sob.

"Over there!" he said, pointing to a cluster of shacks near a rise at the far end of the village.

Motioning the others to follow, he went on. Rough tundra

grass, snow covered and slicked with beads of oil, squelched under his boots as he walked up the slope. Directly facing him was a hut, a hovel, with cracks in the wooden sides and tattered tar paper nailed over holes in the roof. It was in the village but not part of it, isolated on the slope.

He looked back. Harding made a helpless gesture with his shoulders. Millwood walked toward the closed door of the hut, his heart thumping against his chest. He hesitated, tense, listening, yet sure that this was where the cry had come from. Taking a deep breath, he strode forward, yanked down the old-fashioned latch with a sharp click, flung open the door, and stood clear.

For a long moment he squinted into the dark interior, trying to make sense of an obscure form lying on the floor. Slowly it took the shape of a lean and starved-looking dog, lips curled back in a silent snarl, breath seeping in clouds from its nostrils. Front paws hugging the floor in an aggressive posture, the animal lay guarding a wooden bed covered with fur and sealskins. In the bed was a dead Eskimo woman, the old crinkled skin of her face frozen solidly in a portrait of pain. As his eyes became adjusted to the light, he saw the amulet necklace tightly drawn around her neck and, curiously, the scattered rosary beads on the fur covers where her spindly fingers rested like upturned claws.

He turned back to the dog. Cautiously, he extended his hand. The animal tensed. He saw the stained fur, matted and bristly; the eyes, intense and shining, with the edges drawn back along the lids, showing the whites, glinting with a mixture of grief and fear. He had never seen such sadness in a creature's eyes. As he took a step forward, the dog moved toward the bed, sat on its haunches, threw its head back, and uttered a long mournful howl. Then it put its head between its paws and whimpered like a frightened child. Millwood stepped across the threshold, stooped, and patted its head. "There, old buddy," he said in a comforting tone. He crossed to the door, waved to the others, and looked around the room. Newspapers, the cheapest form of insulation, were stuck to the walls. The wind had driven through the weathered boards and formed yellow lines on the paper. On a shelf was an oil lamp, a cracked teapot, a cup, and some crockery. He looked around for the dog's plate. In a corner was a tin dish with a frozen fish on it, untouched.

"It's okay, Eva, he won't bite," he said as she stepped across the threshold and stared at the dog. At the sight of the body on the bed she shuddered and looked away.

"She must have been left behind in the general evacuation," Millwood said.

"What'll we do with her, Captain?" Harding said.

Millwood considered. It wouldn't help morale if they flew the corpse out with them to Dye Main when the weather cleared. On the other hand, they couldn't leave it as it was. They had to give it a decent burial. And there was the dog to consider. It would starve soon. One problem at a time, he thought, dismissing the dog from his mind for the moment.

"We'll bury her here, outside the hut."

"But the ground's frozen, sir," Kelly said.

He looked around, searching for a solution. His eye fastened on a roll of old canvas leaning against the wall.

"We'll wrap her in this," he said, "then dig down as far as we can. Cover it with stones. There's bound to be a spade around. In some of the other houses."

Millwood rested on the spade, watching the dog. It stood with head cast down in utter dejection, eyeing the low mound.

"What'll we do with him, sir?" asked Kelly, throwing down his shovel.

"Let him trail along, if he will," Millwood said. "Now let's find some sleeping quarters."

The door of the Hudson's Bay Company store was locked, but he put his hand through the smashed pane, turned the lock, and went in. In the middle of the floor was a bright yellow snowmobile, the warranty card tied to the chromed steering bar fluttering in the gust of wind that blew through the opening in the door. Behind the counter were shelves with folded blankets, stacks of canned food, bright leather dog harnesses, snowshoes, and rolls of linoleum. Piles of smooth sealskins rose to the ceiling at the back. A treadle-operated sewing machine stood at one side, a piece of heavy red cloth clamped under the needle where someone had demonstrated how the machine worked. On the counter was an unopened package of soap, a carton of eggs, and a package of margarine, frozen solid.

"They left in a hell of a hurry," he said, looking over the shelves again. "Hey, just what we need!" He darted behind the counter and pulled down a sleeping bag. "Harding and Crane, get some others down and then see how much oil's left for the heater. The tank's probably out in back." He snorted. Sixty million gallons of the stuff leaking off the coast, and he was worrying about a few measly gallons to last the night. "We can all sleep here tonight. Get everything ready. Kelly and I will scout around."

The wind had risen. As they walked down the road, he wondered what to do about the dog, which had refused to leave the burial mound. By morning it would probably have frozen to death.

"Straight ahead, Kelly," he said, pointing to the building

near the antenna. The red light at the top glowed against a dark patch in the sky. The generator must still be operating, he thought. Diesel-driven, most likely. He read the inscription over the door—CANADA MINISTRY OF TRANSPORT, METEORO-LOGICAL BRANCH, KIVITOOLUK—and turned the handle. It was locked. "Civil servants!" he said disgustedly. "Lock everything up tight according to the rule book and forget to switch off the bloody generator!" He leaned against the door, testing its security.

"Want me to break it open, Captain?" Kelly said eagerly.

"I'll manage," he growled and threw his body against the panels. He had to do it three times before it flew open. Large weather maps covered the walls. The radio console was at the back. He examined it carefully, located the power switch, and turned it on. There was a hand microphone on a hook. "What's Dye Main's frequency, Kelly? Maybe we can get through with this set. It's got more power than yours."

"Three-five megahertz, sir."

Millwood turned the selector and spoke into the microphone. "Dye Main. Helicopter eight-zero-one. Come in Dye Main. Over!"

The speaker in the center of the console buzzed, but that was all. Not even the thin unintelligible voice.

"Well, it was a try," he said dully, replacing the microphone. The radio operator's log was on the console. He opened it to the last entry and read: *Communication with Dye Main ended 0020 hours. Unable to make outside contact due to blizzard. Everybody making for western Baffin and Frobisher Bay. Station closed down before evacuating.*

Millwood fell silent. Two empty coffee mugs were on the table with several crumpled cigarette packages and an ashtray filled with stubs.

"Let's go," he said, conscious of the flatness of his voice.

On the way back to the center of the village he stopped and looked at the rolling snowdrifts on the plain beyond. A half-buried trail of footsteps and churned-up snow led away. His attention was attracted to a hollow where a patch of yellow and red flowers stood out against the gray background.

"This way," he said.

He bent to examine the delicate blooms spreading above the lichen. The tiny flowers had blossomed in their rush of accelerated growth, cramming their growth cycle into the short burst of Arctic summer. He probed deeply with his finger into the lichen and withdrew it covered with a greasy film. "It must have been one hell of a wind," he said. "What's this?"

"Looks like a miniature tree, sir."

He picked up a limp plant that had been battered to the ground, but was still recognizable as a tree. It reminded him of Japanese bonsai. "My God!" he said. "Some of these plants take over a century to grow. Gone in one oily blizzard!"

"Maybe they'll reseed themselves. Like after forest fires."

Millwood shook his head and pried off a butterfly flattened to the tree's bark by oil globules. He'd read once that in the Arctic it took three years for a caterpillar to become a butterfly. Probably thousands had been destroyed in that one night. He looked for other insects but could find none. Then about thirty yards away, sitting on a large boulder, he saw a snowy owl, staring at him with huge eyes. Its white feathers were stained nearly black with oil. When he stood it spread its wings and flew heavily away, as a raven crossed the sky in the distance.

"It didn't polish off everything, sir," Kelly said cheerfully, watching the bird.

Millwood was silent as they walked back to the trading post. He stopped before a large building, stepped inside the open door, and found himself in a one-room schoolhouse. The desks had been moved against the walls and old blankets put on the floor. "They must have crowded in here to spend the night." He inspected the huge beams supporting the roof. "One of the safest places." His foot struck something: a plastic doll, smashed and dirty, with torn clothing. Nearby was a child's sealskin boot, covered with tar.

"Gives you the creeps, sir."

"Come on, Kelly." He stepped outside, slipped, and fell heavily.

"You okay, sir?"

Millwood sat on the greasy smutch near the doorstep, despair in his heart. It would be a hell of a job to make this place livable again. It might be impossible. They'd need steam, lots of it, to clean off the buildings and the gravel road. And there was the beach. The people had lost everything they owned, and God knew that was little enough:—wooden shacks, a few trapping weapons, and personal possessions. They'd lost it all.

The sudden howl of the dog in the distance made him scramble to his feet. He looked at Kelly.

"See if you can coax him back to the trading post."

"Yes, sir."

Millwood called after him as he set off down the road. "If he won't come, find a gun and finish him off."

He saw Kelly slow and turn around. "You mean it, sir?"

"Yes. He'll freeze to death otherwise." He watched Kelly turn and slowly continue on. Then he walked cautiously down the main road of the village toward the trading post. A morbid curiosity made him peer in at the door of one of the larger houses. He saw the familiar newspapers stuck to the walls, a double bed, children's clothing and a tattered parka hanging from a hook, a double-barreled shotgun on nails driven into the wall. He heard a clock ticking loudly. It was on an upturned orange crate near the bed. There was only one hand, the hour hand, and no glass. He pulled back the sleeve of his parka and checked his watch. Fifteen hundred hours. The bent hand of the clock pointed to approximately the same place on the yellowing dial. He stood like a statue, staring at the clock, unable to take his eyes from it, listening to its merry metallic heartbeat. Apart from the wretched dog, it was the only bit of domestic life left in the village. It would soon need winding to keep it going. At least he could do that. As he stepped forward to pick up the clock, a shot exploded in the clear air and echoed between the rocky hills.

SEVEN

"Some people made it as far as Frobisher," the Dye Main officer said. He got up from the desk and stood in front of a large map of Baffin Island. "These settlements here," he said, sweeping his hand down the coastline, "and up here, north." The deep-set gray eyes were appraising, the lips under the full moustache drawn into a tight line. "Now that radio communication's been restored, the picture's firming up. It's ugly."

The commanding officer sat down, picked up a ruler on the desk with long, elegant fingers, and studied Millwood's rumpled jacket. Millwood tugged at the ends of his sleeves. He tried to wipe away tar stains from the four ribbons of gold braid and shifted uncomfortably in his chair.

"In the Arctic, Captain, news gets around fast—bad news faster. Even without radio."

He's half enjoying this, Millwood realized. The disaster had focused attention on this man and his remote command, and he was making the most of it. It must be dreary here, in the barren wilds of the Arctic, with nothing to do but keep a check on the radarscopes and read the reports brought back by patrolling planes and helicopters. And the horrible feeling at the back of your mind that the Pentagon has forgotten you.

Millwood looked around the room: the carpeted floor, the pleasant wallpaper with the rural motif, a leafy planter in the corner. Through the window of the big quonset hut he saw aircraft parked near the runway and, beyond, other huts and a complex array of antennas set on a bluff overlooking Cape Dyer. Farther out was the ice field, dazzling under a clear blue sky. Two years in this place would drive him nuts. No wonder this man relished the activity starting to take place now that the salvage fleet was coming up the coast. He brought his eyes back to the officer across the desk.

"Other settlements have had to be evacuated, Captain—up here and across there." He swiveled lazily in his chair and pointed with the ruler to the map. "This place, Clyde, hell of a mess there. Weather station's out. And over here, they had to fly out several casualties."

"Casualties, General?"

"Two Eskimos killed when they fell down a crevasse," he said casually. "Several others with broken legs and arms. We flew them down to Frobisher. They've got decent hospital facilities there."

Millwood sucked in a deep breath. The telephone rang.

"General Newton speaking. Yes?"

He turned away and looked out of the window, the telephone to his ear. "How many?" he demanded, smoothing back his moustache. A soldier who wouldn't know one end of a gun from the other, Millwood thought contemptuously.

"Put them in the mess hall. Move the tables together. Put in extra chairs." Newton put down the telephone with a deliberate clatter. "The clean-up experts are going to hold a meeting here," he said importantly. "They're flying in now."

He swung out his arm as though to salute and brought his wrist up before his face with a snap to consult his watch. "They'll be here in fifteen minutes," he announced.

"I'd like to sit in, General."

Newton screwed up his mouth. "I think I can arrange that, Captain," he said pompously, and added condescendingly, "Yes, I think you'd be a useful man to have around."

"The salvage team's coming up the coast now," said the elderly man in the tweed jacket. "When we get their report on *North Star*'s exact position and know how far the spill's spread, we'll have something to work on." He looked around the small group of men sitting at the mess-hall tables. Millwood, sitting opposite, studied the leathery tanned face. When he talked his voice had a tone that Millwood knew would command instant obedience. "Culverton. Vice Admiral, retired," was how he'd introduced himself. Just the bare facts. Enough to let Millwood know who he was, without fuss, without sign of superiority.

"The first satellite picture has come through," he said, pointing to a long roll of paper propped against the wall. He looked at the men seated on each side of him. His eyes rested on Millwood. "I'm glad you could stay, Captain," he said. "You'll be most grateful. What's happened to your crew?"

"I put them on a plane to Boston about an hour ago, sir."

Culverton nodded. His eyes moved on. He pulled together the papers he'd extracted from his briefcase and squared them on the table.

"Gentlemen," he said in a low voice, "this spill is the worst in history. Terms of reference? The same as when we cleaned up Santa Barbara. In two words: scientific coordination. That's our job." He paused, and Millwood got the impression Admiral Culverton and the other scientists shared some special and private experience. Culverton, General Newton had said, basking in reflected glory, was chairman of the President's Panel on Oil Spills, chief scientific adviser to clean-up teams for spills on both sides of the Atlantic, including the *Torrey Canyon* wreck. His work cleaning up the Santa Barbara spill off California, when an undersea oil well blew its top, had been highly praised. Culverton swung around to face Newton.

"Will you please arrange to have the satellite photo pinned up, General, so that we can see it."

Newton, standing stiffly at the end of the room, motioned to a Coast Guard ensign. The young man took the paper roll and pinned it on a blackboard behind the Admiral.

"What altitude was it taken from?" Culverton said.

The ensign studied the notation. "Three hundred and ten miles, sir. At sixteen hundred hours, sir."

Millwood studied the satellite picture. Broad areas of cloud obscured portions of the Baffin Sea. Here and there the coasts of Greenland and Labrador showed through. The Davis Strait was clear. But the sea north of Cape Dyer was enveloped in white and gray clouds, bearing away toward a big black patch farther north.

"Doesn't show much," said a young man with curly fair hair and a straggly beard who sat opposite. His tone, Millwood thought, implied disgust.

"It's only the first picture, Dr. Meschino," Culverton said quietly. "One thing at a time. How's that bacteria experiment of yours coming along?"

Meschino's face brightened. "The final report on the first experiments is almost ready. The latest batch had voracious appetites."

"The pseudomonas?"

"Yes. The population growth within forty-eighty hours

jumped from ten thousand micro-organisms per milliliter to twenty million."

"And the breakdown?"

"Between fifty and seventy per cent of the oil breaks down into harmless components. I'm pleased with the results so far."

The Admiral turned from Meschino and looked around the room. "This must sound mysterious to some of the non-technical types here," he said without condescension. "Dr. Meschino's talking about bacteria he's trained to eat oil."

Millwood blinked. "That's fantastic, sir," he said.

"We think so too. The little buggers work twenty-four hours a day without pay, no time off for sick leave, and no labor problems."

"I've heard of bacteria leaching mine tailings," Millwood said.

"Yes, that's the same thing," Meschino said with sudden interest, turning to Millwood.

"Does it work on crude oil, Dr. Meschino?" Millwood said.

It was as if a light had been switched off inside Meschino's head. His face went blank. Millwood realized he'd put a question better left unasked. Meschino looked quickly at the Admiral. "So far——" but the Admiral cut him off.

"Works very effectively on marine diesel oil, Captain. But crude is—so far—difficult for them to digest. That about sums it up, wouldn't you say, Dr. Meschino?"

"Exactly," Meschino said. He turned to the Admiral as though for protection. "The freeze-drying experiments are shaping up, too."

"Dr. Meschino and his associate microbiologists at the Navy Civil Engineering Lab are working on an idea to stockpile bacteria by a special freeze-drying process. The idea is to dump them on a spill from the air. However"—Culverton looked at the big blowup of the satellite photograph—"I don't think we can count on bacteria to help us here. The water's too cold."

"I've ordered some Prudhoe Bay crude to be shipped to the labs," Meschino said brightly. "I want to develop a bacteria strain that will break down the molecular structure."

"Good," said a little fat man next to the Admiral.

Millwood glanced at him, a rotund man with metal-rimmed glasses, pudgy hands clasped together on the table. He tried to remember his name—Essenhicker or something like that. Dr. Essenhigh, that was it. Chief physics man on the scientific team. Next to him was a tall, gaunt man. Doctor or Mister? Millwood racked his brain. The introductions had been made so quickly when the team had flown into Dye Main that he'd lost track.

"Dr. Matheson," the Admiral said. "How much peat moss and straw on board the salvage fleet?"

"Five hundred tons, Admiral."

"The Navy's a bit optimistic, aren't they?" He stuck out his lower lip. "Good for about five square miles, with luck," he said gloomily. "We'll have to do better than that." He turned to Millwood. "Captain, how much oil was left in the cargo tanks when you abandoned *North Star?*"

Millwood was conscious of the faces turned in his direction. "We had sixty million gallons aboard when we sailed from Prudhoe." He took a deep breath. "I estimate we lost a third by the time I abandoned ship." He felt as though he was in the prisoner's box in a crowded courtroom. The faces staring at him were weighing him, accusing.

"Forty million gallons still aboard, eh?" The Admiral bent his head, made a few swift movements with a slide rule. "Forty gallons of crude, under certain conditions, will cover more than ten acres of sea. So forty million gallons would

cover ten million acres." He manipulated the slide rule and
looked up gravely. "Fifteen thousand square miles!"

It hit Millwood like a hammerblow. Fifteen thousand
square miles! It would cover the whole of Baffin Bay. And
there were the other twenty million already lost—mostly
under the ice—farther north.

"That's being unrealistic." Matheson's voice was shrill.
"That would only happen if she sinks."

"Sinks?" Millwood said weakly.

"Forget it!" said Culverton. "He's being pessimistic! Now,
gentlemen, let's go over the details."

Millwood stared at the latest satellite photoprint the Admiral
unrolled on the table. The clouds over the Baffin Sea had
vanished. A widespread dark patch covered the lighter tone
indicating water. He looked over the tops of the bent heads.

"Across the entire bay and down as far as Cape Dyer,"
Culverton said in low tones. "The Labrador Current'll soon
get hold of it. There'll be hell to pay if it gets away—down
south here!" He swept his pencil down the Labrador coast
toward Newfoundland and the Atlantic shipping lanes. "I
can't understand how it spread so fast." He passed a hand
through his thin white hair.

"We need a fast peat moss airdrop, sir," Matheson said.
"Let's get the helicopters off to drop loads on the southern
front. Help soak it up. Slow it down. But we'd have to clean
it up later with a wire mesh screen. That's what they tried
out successfully after the Arrow sank off Nova Scotia."

Essenhigh thumped the table. "Peat moss won't soak it up
fast enough! Use urethane foam."

"It's only been used experimentally on very small spills."

"Heated urethane ejected from a nozzle in a low-flying
airplane will cover the area quicker than moss. Time's
against us." Essenhigh's gravelly voice was defiant.

The Admiral put up his hand. "General Newton," he said, "where's the latest met report? For the whole of Baffin Bay."

"Immediately, Admiral." Newton crossed to a telephone and dialed, drawing Millwood's eyes to the window. It was bright outside. The sun shone from a clear sky. At least the weather was in their favor. He wondered how near the salvage fleet was to *North Star*. The door opened, and a Coast Guard lieutenant entered, holding a sheet of paper.

"I'll take it," Culverton said curtly, grabbing the paper from the man's hand. He studied the teletyped sheet intently. "Here's a bit of luck. High pressure ridge over Greenland. A ten-knot easterly wind over Baffin. Clearing skies in the north."

"Thank God for that," said a lean man.

"Thank God is right, Mr. Arnold," Culverton replied. "Any word from Ottawa yet?"

"No, sir. But as the official Canadian government representative, I can assure you that every assistance will be forthcoming."

The Admiral looked amused. "That's reassuring," he said. He turned to Matheson. "Radio the clean-up fleet. Order an airdrop of two hundred tons of peat moss at the southern front of the spill. Get a report on the wind velocity and surface conditions at the same time."

Matheson reached for the telephone and began talking into it. Culverton went on. "In the meantime, we'd better knock around a few ideas. We're up against water at near freezing point and ice-covered water and——"

"We haven't discussed a burn-off, sir," Essenhigh cut in.

"It was tried on the *Arrow*. Didn't have much success," Meschino said gloomily.

"The biggest problem is getting the flames going fast and furious," Culverton said. "It was cold in Chedabucto Bay. The water acted as a heat sink, absorbing the heat from the flames. They just died off. I was aboard the *Compton* off Yarmouth when they did burn trials. They got a firestorm going but——"

"That wasn't crude oil! It was used on thin Bunker C." Millwood blurted out uncontrollably. He felt his cheeks flush.

"Right," said the Admiral, unperturbed. "Not crude." He turned to Essenhigh. "What about emulsified oil? That's one hell of a problem." Millwood felt relieved attention had been drawn from him.

"To burn off?" Essenhigh said.

"Yes. What's the latest?"

"A German company's developed a paste containing calcium carbide and metallic sodium as active ingredients. It self-ignites when you drop it on oil. Like napalm. They burned off about ten tons of Arabian crude in a demonstration in the North Sea. I saw it. We should contact them."

"Only ten tons!" Meschino jumped up. "We're talking two hundred thousand tons!"

"Burning's still in an experimental stage," Essenhigh said. "Nobody's had any real success so far. But it's worth trying. Here. I'll read you what they said about *Arrow.*" He plunged his hand into a bulging briefcase and pulled out a slim paper-covered report. "Here's *Operation Oil*, the official report on the *Arrow* cleanup. Here's what it says about burn-offs. Blah-blah-blah, ah, here. 'These experiences show the need for further research and development on methods of burning oil slicks. In cases of oil spills, in isolated areas or amidst ice' "—he flashed a dark look at Meschino—" 'burning may be one of a few methods of control.' Then it goes on to discuss some lab experiments."

Meschino snorted. Culverton looked at him severely. Millwood had the impression the Admiral was dealing with a familiar quarrel. "That brings us back to absorption and containment," Culverton said.

"We haven't discussed floating booms and air curtains," Essenhigh snapped.

Culverton put the palms of his hands upward. "Go ahead, Dr. Essenhigh. What's the latest on booms and curtains?"

Essenhigh drew himself up, puffed out his cheeks, and cleared his throat noisily, reminding Millwood of a fat frog preparing to croak.

"There's been some useful work done with a fine seine net with Bunker C in frigid water. Retains the oil effectively, especially if you throw in peat moss to absorb the oil."

Meschino raised his eyebrows contemptuously.

"Go on, Dr. Essenhigh," Culverton said pleasantly. "The air curtain didn't work very effectively at Santa Barbara. Any improvements since?"

"It was the heavy seas. But if it stays calm"—Essenhigh jerked his balding head toward the window—"it might be worth a try. They've made a rubberized boom now with more holes. That means more air bubbles rise to the surface to cut off the oil."

"Bunker C," Meschino said in a flat tone.

Essenhigh stopped, turned to Culverton, and said, "Air bubbles are worth bearing in mind." Culverton nodded. Millwood heard a helicopter approach and pass overhead.

"The conveyor-belt machine that licks up the oil is something else again. There's a pollution equipment company that's developed a machine to pick up more than fifty gallons a minute. We could use several of them with a mechanical boom around this southern front." He pointed his stubby finger at the map. "It would slow down the——"

The door burst open. A Coast Guard lieutenant entered carrying a paper roll. He addressed the Admiral. "Just came in, sir. The latest satellite picture."

Culverton quickly unrolled the photoprint onto the table. The edge of the spill had moved noticeably farther south.

"It's moving damned fast!" Meschino exclaimed.

Culverton was silent as he studied the picture. He checked his watch. After a long moment he looked up. "We'll wait for the report from the salvage helicopters."

"At this rate we'll soon see it from here, off the Cape," Essenhigh said despondently. "The spill must be a hundred miles long by now."

"I can arrange air transport, sir," Newton interjected from the end of the table, "if you want to inspect it yourself."

Culverton raised his hand. "Thank you, General. That won't be necessary. For the time being anyway."

"But look at this, sir! And this!" Essenhigh said, jabbing at two slicks on the map that had broken from the main spill and were curling toward Davis Strait. "It's spreading like wildfire! We'll never contain it if we delay!"

"Our first point of attack is here, sir," Meschino said, bringing his hand down with a karate chop on the map. Millwood inspected the point at the leading edge of the spill.

"If we wait longer it'll emulsify and disperse. Too late to get the bugs working on it. They work best on neat oil. Water in the oil slows them down." He paused and muttered, "I wish to God we could just bundle it up and tow it away!"

"If bugs are the answer," Essenhigh said, his voice rising.

"Gentlemen," Culverton said quietly with a warning edge to his voice, "keep the fighting for the oil. Heaven knows we're going to need it." He sat down and motioned for the others to sit also. When he had their full attention he said: "We're going to need ingenious methods, using all known techniques and probably new ones we'll devise as we proceed. As soon as *North Star*'s located, we'll make a decision on our main point of attack and the methods we'll use. We won't gain anything by rushing in and doing a half-assed job. It's got to be an absolutely coordinated scheme, first to contain, second to absorb, and third to remove the oil. When that's done, we'll tackle the damage up the coast, in the villages and settlements. Captain Millwood says there's an Eskimo settlement called Kivitoo. . . ."

"Kivitooluk," Millwood said.

"Kivitooluk. It's been completely abandoned. The blizzard picked up emulsified oil and rained it down on the place. General Newton says Clyde's been evacuated, and other places farther north have been seriously damaged. But the land clean-up will have to wait until we've controlled the spill at sea. In the meantime——"

The wall telephone rang shrilly. Newton hurried to answer it. He picked up the receiver. Whoever was at the other end was excited. Millwood could hear an indistinct shrill voice six feet away. He saw Newton stiffen, his face whitening. "I'll tell the Admiral immediately," he said hoarsely, jamming the telephone back into its cradle. He turned to Culverton.

"It's *North Star*, sir. She sank in twelve hundred feet of water!"

EIGHT

"This is CBS News, New York. The weirdly colored sunrise observed this morning was caused by the oil spill now swirling south from the Labrador Sea. Today, early-morning risers in Manhattan got a clear view of the yellow, green, blue, red, and purple sunrise that scientists at the Woods Hole Oceanographic Institution say was caused by the refraction of light from the sun on the oil, now drifting in the Labrador Current past Newfoundland and into Atlantic shipping lanes."

Millwood caught the eye of the operator at the console in the radio shack. The operator turned up the volume control. "New York's loud and clear today, Captain," he said, and turned to attend to his switch panel. Through the window beyond, Millwood saw the flotilla of Coast Guard cutters and Navy destroyers anchored off the Cape Dyer headland. Farther out, oil slicks curled southward.

"Aerial reconnaissance of the spill and photographs taken by United States weather satellites show that the leading edge of the spill is now centered over the Mid Ocean Canyon, south of Greenland. Marine authorities are concerned that the oil may be picked up by the Gulf Stream and carried east across the Atlantic."

Millwood groaned. The thing he most dreaded was happening.

"Remain tuned to this network for the weather and a taped interview with Dr. Silvester R. Ryckman of Princeton University, who will explain just what's happening out there in the Atlantic."

"He's good," the operator called. "Heard him once talking about the continental drift. An oceanographer and ecologist."

Millwood listened to the end of the newscast with growing frustration. Pilots returning to Dye Main had reported the spill had spread across the narrowest part of Davis Strait from Cape Dyer to Greenland, and south to the Newfoundland coast. He wondered about the offshore and inshore fishing industries in Newfoundland, remembering the time he'd put in to St. John's after the Second World War and seen the hundreds of Portuguese fishermen in white longliners preparing to sail for the Grand Banks, where they had fished for centuries. In a moment of reflection he again walked on that dockside, looking at the decks ablaze with red and yellow dory sails hanging up to dry, the colorful trawl buoys slung high on the masts, the flags emblazoned with the Portuguese coat-of-arms rippling in the breeze from the Narrows that led to the broad blue Atlantic beyond. He recalled chatting with Captain Toscano of the *Gil Eannes*, flagship of the fleet, as she lay at berth alongside. As many as six thousand Portuguese fishermen, he learned, worked on the Grand Banks and as far north as the southern tip of Greenland. There had been more than seventy longliners with hundreds of dories stacked like saucers on the decks. Across the harbor had been moored British and Spanish ships. He knew that many Japanese, Scandinavian, German, and Russian vessels fished the Grand Banks too.

"And now here is Dr. Silvester R. Ryckman of Princeton to talk about the significance of the spill. He is interviewed by Robert H. Boehmer, science correspondent of *The New York Times*."

The radio operator moved to the clattering teletype machine and tore off a long sheet of paper. He studied the sheet and handed it to an officer sitting in a cubicle at the far end of the room. Millwood saw him reach for a telephone.

"Dr. Ryckman, how does this oil spill compare with others? Is it something really big or are the reports exaggerated?"

"There's been nothing to compare with this spill. It's the worst in marine history."

"As an oceanographer and ecologist, would you care to comment on what's likely to happen to the East Coast of the United States as a result of the spill?"

"That's hard to say at this point. In the first place, the oil may be carried in the opposite direction, easterly across the Atlantic, where it could pollute the coasts of Britain, France, and perhaps even Norway."

"How's that?"

"At the moment the spill is collected in a giant swirl about eleven hundred miles directly east of Boston. At that point, called the Mid Ocean Canyon, as you heard on the news report a minute ago, the Gulf Stream moves up. It forms the North Atlantic Current, flowing in a northeasterly direction past the British Isles, where it becomes the Norway Current. If it gets that far——"

"Aren't you being pessimistic, Dr. Ryckman?"

"No, no, I think not. Do you know how much oil has been released from the submarine tanker since she sank? At least— and I emphasize at least—twenty million gallons. There's another twenty million gallons left in the hull, and still leaking, rising to the surface. By comparison, the *Torrey Canyon*——"

"That was the British tanker wrecked on a reef off the Scilly Isles in . . . uh . . . 1967, I think."

134

"Yes. In 1967, that's right. . . . Well, by comparison, she lost twenty-two million gallons, and it was a week before the British managed to do something to prevent the oil spreading. By that time it was too late and you know what happened."

"The English and French coasts were polluted for hundreds of miles, including some of their best resort beaches."

"Yes. So you see, this *North Star* disaster is the worst yet."

"Speaking as an ecologist, what would you expect to happen now? Assuming they can't stop the oil spreading. What happens then?"

"These colored sunrises we've been observing are the key to it."

"How d'you mean—the key?"

"The peculiar colors of the sunrise are due to the refraction of the sun's light as it comes in at a low angle over the ocean. But an important point, one that's not been mentioned so far, is that the vast area of polar seas farther north covered with black oil is creating a huge heat sink. The black area, which used to be white, remember, with ice floes, is absorbing the sun's heat and will cause large areas of ice to melt. This in turn will raise the level of water in Baffin Bay. The result is that the water from these polar regions will flow—it already may have begun—down into the Atlantic faster than normal, and in greater volume."

"Are we going to be flooded? Here in New York?"

"Oh, no, I'm not suggesting we're going to be flooded, not in New York anyway. But there'll be a definite rise in the level of the Atlantic, small but significant. This spill should be a warning to us. Meddling with the polar regions could have dire consequences."

"What do you mean precisely?"

"If a sizable portion of the ice cap should melt and increase the natural southerly flow of ocean water from the

135

Arctic, then we can expect problems with tide levels in New York, or Boston, or anywhere down the eastern seaboard. At the least, beaches would vanish and many docks would have to be rebuilt to accommodate the new higher levels. At the worst . . . well, it could be catastrophic."

"Are you being pessimistic now, Dr. Ryckman?"

"No, still realistic. But conjectural, I'll admit. On the other hand, there's an unconfirmed report that the water level in Portugal Cove in Conception Bay, Newfoundland, has risen substantially in the past week. We've discussed the significance of this at Princeton, and Woods Hole has sent a scientific team to make on-the-spot observations and measurements."

"How far is 'risen substantially'?"

"Two feet above normal."

"Caused by the oil spill?"

"Indirectly. The ice on Davis Strait has begun to melt much earlier this season due to the oil covering large areas of it. The International Iceberg Patrol reports smaller icebergs in southern latitudes."

"You mean the icebergs have melted earlier in the season than usual?"

"Yes."

"What do you think has happened to Portugal Cove?"

"I hope the rise in water level's due to the channeling effect of the Bay. The cove's halfway up the bay, and there's a large island, Wabana, offshore. I think that as the higher-than-normal tide swept up the bay, it was squeezed between the island and the mainland and got channeled into the cove. That might be a reasonable explanation for the rise. Two feet above normal is, putting it mildly, a substantial increase."

"Are there other reports of high tides, Doctor?"

"I haven't heard of any. It's possible the coordinator of the task force knows of more."

"Admiral Culverton, in charge at Cape Dyer disaster headquarters?"

"Yes. We at Princeton and Woods Hole are working with him."

"Doing what?"

"Instantaneous research, if you'll pardon the expression. This thing can't wait. We're working on problems as they arise. If the task force can't contain the spill, we've simply got to curtail its effects."

"Can you tell our listeners something about the sort of research you are doing now?"

"The most important work is on strains of bacteria that eat oil. Some years ago it was discovered that certain bacteria absorb oleic materials. We at the labs are trying to breed bacteria that consume crude oil, specifically Prudhoe Bay crude oil."

"How are the experiments progressing, Doctor?"

"Encouraging."

"How encouraging?"

"Encouraging, that's all I'm prepared to say at the moment."

"Well, what I mean is: Can we expect to see the spill cleaned up by your new breed of bugs? I mean——"

"Encouraging. Nothing more. I uh——"

"Yes?"

"I was going to add: Whatever the end result of cleaning up the spill, it'll be a combination of several different methods. Pseudomonas, if the experiments prove fruitful, will be only one of them."

"Let's get back to the ecology angle. I know you have a

personal interest in conservation and nature. What will happen up north, on the Labrador coast and Newfoundland, if the oil gets ashore there?"

"Sheer disaster! *Great* damage to the ecology."

"What sort of damage?"

"You've heard about what happened on Baffin Island. How the Eskimo settlements were affected. It will be the same farther south. Miles of beaches will be fouled. No doubt about that. With serious effects on wildlife."

"What about fishing?"

"I was coming to that. I'm concerned about the Grand Banks. If the oil swings west, it'll do irreparable damage to the fishing grounds—"

"I'm sorry to interrupt you, Doctor, but our time is up.

"That was an interview with Dr. Silvester R. Ryckman of Princeton University talking with Robert H. Boehmer of *The New York Times.* Back to our scheduled broadcast in a moment. Here is a special announcement. Don't forget to see the specially televised program that starts at six o'clock tomorrow morning, in color, of the new sunrise over New York."

Millwood caught a whiff of oil in the plane's air-conditioning system. He looked over the pilot's shoulder. The altimeter hovered just under five hundred feet. Broken floes zipped past below, covered with scum. The big turboprop flew on with engines throttled back, its broad-bladed propellers flashing lazily in the sunlight. Culverton pointed. Directly ahead lay the salvage fleet, three cutters that fussed around a fleet of ocean tugs. Millwood could see the jibs of cranes projecting beyond the decks of the tugs. Orange marker buoys showed up brightly against the oil. As they flew over, he saw faces looking up and, in the center of the flotilla, a dense black turbulence where *North Star*'s cargo bubbled to the surface.

"They're trying to plug the bow," the Admiral said.

"What submersible are they using?" Essenhigh asked.

"*Tracker Two.* She's got a working depth of six thousand feet. If she can't do it, nothing will."

"Too damned late now!" Meschino said. "Shutting the stable door after the horse has gone." He made a helpless gesture.

The aircraft turned, swept back over the scene of activity below, and headed south. Culverton got up from his seat near Millwood and stood in the open doorway of the flight deck. Millwood heard the pilot say: "It's about eighty minutes to the southern front, sir. Do you want to view it close to the surface or stay at five thousand feet?"

"Five thousand," the Admiral said decisively. He returned to his seat in the austere cabin. Millwood looked out of the window. The plane was climbing steeply. In a few minutes it leveled off. Millwood gasped. The oil spread across the ocean as far as he could see. He looked through the window on the opposite side of the cabin. The surface was a greenish black, irridescent under the bright sunlight. Large gray ice floes spotted parts of the sea, like obscure animals herding together for mutual protection. Through his own window, due east, was the distant silvery edge of the ice field off the Greenland coast. He wondered whether the oil had whipped up over the ice field during the recent blizzard. The desolate scene at Kivitooluk swept through his mind.

"Coffee, Captain?"

The crewman jolted his thoughts. He took the plastic cup of steaming liquid.

"Thanks." He pushed away the cream and sugar.

"Hey, look over there!" Meschino shouted, jumping up and spilling his coffee.

Millwood crossed to Meschino's window. Coming up on the

plane's path were several icebergs, in a ragged line astern formation, tops glittering in the sun, their sides sculptured into fantastic shapes by the wind. They shone with dazzling radiance from a corrugated ebony sea, like diamonds scattered across rippled black velvet.

"Lose height!" Culverton barked at the pilot.

The icebergs gave the illusion of being stationary, locked in the inky water. As the plane came down in a slowly descending spiral, Millwood could see the prematurely rounded edges of the icebergs where they had begun to melt. The sun's heat had been absorbed by the oil and the nearby water warmed as a result.

"Over there!" Essenhigh shouted, pointing.

The whine of the engines died as the throttles were pulled back. When they leveled off, Millwood saw a stranded polar bear on an outlying shelf of the iceberg.

"It'll be a race against time for him," the Admiral said. "If the berg melts before it gets out of this muck. . . ."

The bear's head swiveled from side to side as the plane flew alongside a hundred feet away. In a few seconds they were past and climbing. Squinting against the sun's reflection off the sea, Millwood could make out an outline of silvery water ahead. In a moment or two he saw the edge of the spill, open water edged in blue, dotted with small ice cakes. Then he saw the helicopters, Sikorsky CH-53s and Sky Cranes, blades whirling as they flew low over the southern front of the spill. Above cruised four-engined transport planes and, above them, several twin-engined aircraft from which the massive airdrop of peat moss was being directed. Bundles curved down from the big transports and splashed into the water, spread out along the front of the advancing spill, quickly turning a muddy color as the moss sucked up the oil.

The airplane turned to starboard, and he was looking down

on scores of ships forming an arc spread across several miles of ocean, a thin black thread connecting them. The thread and ships stretched to the horizon.

"The boom," Essenhigh called across the aisle.

"But why there? There's no oil."

"Head it off at the pass!" Meschino grinned. "See. Down there. That destroyer . . . no, it's a cutter. A big one. She's at the center, lead ship, giving instructions on how to lay out the boom on each side."

"They're spreading the boom already, for the oil when it comes south?"

The Admiral nodded. "If it holds we'll suck up the oil to the north of it," he said.

"How long will the boom be?" Millwood said.

"Seventy miles."

"Seventy miles! Can it stand the pressure?"

Essenhigh shook his head. "We've made deliberate breaks in it. Every five miles. To let the oil escape and relieve the pressure. See, there's a break, about a mile that way. Those ships clustered around the break will suck up the oil as it slips through the gap. They've got conveyor belt suckers on board."

"Seventy miles!" Millwood repeated.

"The longest boom that's ever been tried," the Admiral said.

"What's it made of?" Millwood asked.

"Chain link fencing laced through with a thick steel cable to take the strain. Those are empty sealed oil drums you see about every fifty feet to support it on the surface."

"Chain link fencing!"

"Yes—ordinary garden fencing. They tried it when the *Arrow* went down. Works well. We've tied fir tree boughs to the fencing. The fir needles absorb the oil."

"Really?"

"The needles form a sort of membrane. Lets the water through but holds the oil back," Culverton said in a matter-of-fact tone. "We're also trying an air curtain boom in a few places to see if it works on a large scale."

About a hundred ships, old trampers, battered trawlers and a ragged fleet of rusty lighters, were arranged in line abreast formation. The aircraft swung low over them, low enough for Millwood to see ropes over their bows.

"There's the bubble curtain," Meschino said, crossing to Millwood's side and pointing. "Those ropes overboard keep the curtain on station below the surface. See, the mechanical boom's ahead of it."

It didn't seem possible that a jet of air bubbles and a narrow boom could hold back the drift of oil. The spill spread far to east and west and must be at least five hundred miles from north to south. It would take more than a thin defense line like this to stop it. Surely defense in depth was needed. Millwood wondered about the scientists' ability to cope.

The pilot called back, "This is the end of the line so far as the spill goes, Admiral. Do you want to fly down the line of ships?"

"No. I'm satisfied with what's going on here. I want to see down south," Culverton said.

"Right, sir. South it is."

The line of ships fell astern. A line of cumulus clouds hugged the southern horizon. The shadow of the wing fell across Millwood's arm as the airplane banked and set off on a new course. The engine roar rose in volume. He felt the thrust as the speed increased. Except for tiny specks of white that were ice cakes, the sea was clear. He crossed to the starboard side and sat behind Meschino. A faint smudge lay on the western horizon.

"Labrador coast," he said over the chair top to Meschino.

"Either that or Newfoundland, Captain."

"Newfie," the Admiral said, showing a map he'd unfolded on his lap. "Reports of high tides there already. My God, that's a new one!"

Millwood stared below. An oil slick about half a mile long had appeared directly below, curving in a crescent. "That didn't show up on the satellite pictures. What the hell?" said Culverton.

"Cloud cover, sir?" Meschino suggested.

Culverton was silent, his heavy shoulders slouched as he bent over the map. "It's about here," he said, tracing his finger over the map in the region of the Newfoundland coast.

"The Grand Banks, sir," said Millwood, looking over Culverton's shoulder. "Is there a possibility——"

"A very distinct possibility, Captain." He got up and went forward. The aircraft banked and headed off on a new bearing. Culverton returned to his seat. "We're going northeast for a bit. Check if there're more slicks headed toward mid-Atlantic."

Millwood peered at the sea. There was a ground swell urged on by a strong westerly wind on the surface, and he recognized the deeper undulations of waves that had fetched for great distances across the ocean deeps. The line of cumulus to the south had come closer, indicating they were in a high-pressure region. At least that was something in their favor. He peered ahead and his gut tightened. Coming up was a great slick that flattened the swell. He saw the Admiral check the map.

"The confluence of the Gulf Stream and the Labrador Current. It's what I figured. Blasted stuff's escaped from the main spill!"

Millwood stared below. Tentacles of oil coiled off the slick and drifted languidly in great spindly arms. The plane went lower. He sniffed the sickly smell as fumes flushed through the cabin air-conditioning system. A wing tilted. He lay poised directly over the oily scum until the plane leveled off and headed away. Culverton got up and went to the flight deck.

"We'll take a look at the Grand Banks," he said, coming back.

The sea cleared, but after a few minutes a sudden mist obscured the surface. Low clouds flicked past the window. They were in thick fog. The engine sound increased. In a few seconds they were in sunlight and suddenly the fog below parted and dozens of small boats bobbed on the surface in the company of big white ships. He recognized them instantly; dories and longliners of the Portuguese Great White Fleet. The fog clamped down and the ships vanished.

When it cleared again the sea was clear. Two trawlers skimmed below the wing, followed by a big black ship flying a white flag with a large red dot in the center, a Japanese factory ship.

"The Grand Banks." Meschino said. "They're clear!"

The Admiral was engrossed in the map. "Fly fifteen minutes due west, then head north," he shouted to the flight deck.

The fog had cleared and the sea sparkled. It stretched away to the south in a limitless expanse. It seemed crazy to think that only an hour's flying time due north there was a huge sea of oil covering this beauty. Millwood suddenly yearned to be on his old Navy submarine, cutting through the brilliant sea, heading into the broad Atlantic on one of those NATO exercises he used to enjoy.

He wondered what Eva was doing. Perhaps she was already back in the Navy's electronics experimental labs. The plane banked, tipping his thoughts back to reality.

"We're heading for Dyer," Meschino said.

The Newfoundland coast showed up again, a low russet line as the sun caught the distant cliffs. He wondered about the significance of the high tide at Portugal Cove. As he brooded, the crewman came forward with another tray of steaming coffee cups. He stopped at Millwood's elbow. Millwood helped himself. "Thanks," he grunted and peered out of the window, staring gloomily at the distant coastline.

NINE

Culverton put down the telephone. "Captain Reed in the control cutter reports oil at the boom," he said. "Everything's holding."

"Keep your fingers crossed!" Essenhigh muttered. The Admiral's eyes glinted. He turned to Meschino.

"What's doing with the bacteria?"

"A sample of Prudhoe crude's been airlifted from Alaska."

"Christ!" Essenhigh exploded. "Are you serious? "Thirty million gallons of it drifting past the window, and they fly it in from Prudhoe!"

Meschino's bearded jaw stuck out defiantly. "Bureaucrats at the labs. What d'you expect?"

"Stupid bastards!" Culverton snapped. It was the first time he'd shown irritation since the crisis had developed. During the past two days at headquarters, giving instructions to ships at sea, arranging reconnaissance flights, making sure peat moss was dropped at the right places at the right times, Culverton had kept calm. When bickering broke out he'd smoothed ruffled feelings with tact and diplomacy. But Millwood had

146

noticed the twitching mouth, the deepening lines around it, the clenching fingers whenever the telephone rang.

"It's done now," Meschino said philosophically. "They've started work on them."

"How long before we get results?" Matheson demanded.

"Three or four days."

"Four days!" Essenhigh thumped the table. "If that damned boom breaks. . . ." He paused, drumming his fingers on the table, "I'm going to move some of the conveyor belt ships up closer, to relieve pressure on the boom."

"What about the peat-moss distribution?" Culverton asked.

"I'm dropping another hundred loads at the southern end. They're still working it back toward the north."

The telephone rang shrilly. The Admiral picked up the receiver. "Culverton," he announced, so softly that Millwood, at the end of the table, could hardly hear him. Then he said, "Oh, God!"

He replaced the receiver and looked around the room. "They've abandoned *North Star*. *Tracker Two* got fouled in the oil. Impossible to get near the sub's bow."

There was a stunned silence. By some miracle of self-control, Millwood managed to keep his feelings in check. How he hated sitting around this table, listening to these scientists chatting about bugs and moss, like women exchanging snippets of housekeeping lore. He watched Culverton, bent over the latest satellite map on the table, biting his lip. Culverton's was essentially an overview, Millwood reflected, but by some osmotic process, the Admiral's own sense of despair came through to Millwood.

Matheson's voice cut into his thoughts. "I'll tell the ships at the boom. The pressure will go on increasing until the rest of the cargo escapes."

RAGE UNDER THE ARCTIC

Perhaps he'd misjudged these men, Millwood thought. Their exchange of views, their listening to the latest radio reports, minutely examining satellite photographic blowups, weighing facts, calculating data, were responsible for the actions of thousands of men spread over hundreds of square miles of oil-covered ocean, for the control of crews of scores of ships, hundreds of clean-up experts now scanning the spill from dozens of helicopters, men aboard the big transport planes dumping peat moss and chemicals to absorb the oil, photographic analysts at NASA in Houston marking satellite photographs with coded computerized numerals and gridded lines, indicating with remarkable accuracy the encroaching spill south of Davis Strait, measuring its velocity, surface pressure, and temperature from infra-red cameras and spectrometric apparatus hundreds of miles in space.

His sense of loss at abandoning *North Star*, and the damage at Kivitooluk and farther north, had warped his opinion of the others. Their offhand manner, he realized now, was a shield consciously adopted to keep a check on their own emotions. Even Essenhigh, a temperamental firebrand, had kept his feelings under tight rein. Millwood had no reason to doubt General Newton's word, when he'd told him Essenhigh was the most brilliant physicist in oil clean-up technology in the United States. Meschino was his opposite in chemical science, and Matheson was the most advanced man in environmental damage control.

Matheson was speaking into the telephone. "Pressure will build up at the boom as the rate of flow increases." Matheson took a small book of mathematical tables from his pocket and ran a ballpoint pen down the columns. "Give me a shout if the wind down there either veers or backs more than three points. What's it doing now?" Matheson cocked his thin head as he listened, eyes half shut in concentration. "That's good news, at any rate." He put down the receiver and turned to Culverton. "The ships at the ends of the boom report that the wind's dying now, sir. But the oil pressure's increased. What do you think?"

The Admiral looked at Essenhigh. "Beef up your boom with a reserve boom."

"Right—and put in a secondary boom a half-mile south," Essenhigh agreed. "We haven't got much time."

Culverton nodded. Essenhigh picked up a telephone. "Get Captain Reed on Coast Guard Cutter seven-four-two," he said.

"Captain Reed? It's Essenhigh at Dye Main. They can't plug *North Star*, so get prepared to meet the full pressure of forty million gallons of oil at the boom. You probably picked up Dr. Matheson's conversation with the boom-end vessels. Hold on, Captain, while I work it out for you."

Essenhigh studied the satellite map, moving his finger across it, still speaking into the telephone.

"The temperature at the boom is thirty-three degrees Fahrenheit. You can double-check that. Hold on."

He laid down the receiver, made a rapid movement with his slide rule, and jotted down some figures, then picked up the receiver.

"There'll be a pressure of approximately one hundred and sixty thousand tons of oil distributed along the length of the boom, the whole seventy-mile length. We want a secondary boom constructed half a mile south. Repeat: half a mile south. What's your position?"

Millwood saw the sudden crinkling of the lines around the fat man's eyes. The thick lower lip jutted out. Essenhigh pulled a large handkerchief from his trouser pocket and daubed his forehead. "Oh, the Navy! You'll get an okay from headquarters?" Essenhigh sucked in his breath and seemed to swell up until Millwood thought he would burst. The little man turned to the Admiral. "Captain Reed says he'll have to ask the Navy. They've requisitioned all reserve supplies of boom sections."

"Give me that phone!" Culverton grabbed the instrument so savagely Millwood thought he'd yank Essenhigh's arm off. "What's going on down there!" Culverton listened with mounting impatience. "Stand by, Captain Reed," he barked. "I'll be back directly." He stabbed the telephone button impatiently. "Hello, Dye Main operator? Get me Washington. The Chief of Naval Operations. Top priority call!" He waited for the connection to be made.

Millwood heard the water drip from the roof as the snow from the recent storm melted. The sun must be strong now that it was midday. Surprising how the warmth penetrated and accumulated in the sheltered spaces on a summer day north of the Arctic Circle. The Eskimo village fastened itself on his mind, and he wondered if any of the people had returned. It hardly seemed likely: Matheson was too busy with the oil at sea to do anything about cleaning up the coastal regions. The land clean-up would have to wait. If they got a Navy supply vessel up through the inlet and ran pipes ashore, they could steam the oil off the beach and gravel roads. But there'd be no point in trying to clean the houses. They'd have to burn them down and start again.

Culverton's voice put an abrupt end to his speculating. "Admiral, this is Admiral Culverton at Dye Main. I need your help, sir. I *have* to construct a new boom—I must put one in half a mile south of the existing one. To act as a reserve in case the first boom fails under the full pressure now that we know they can't plug *North Star*." He listened for a moment. "The Navy's requisitioned every existing yardage of boom section not in use, Admiral. But the Coast Guard needs them *now*." Another pause. A purple flush began to spread upward from the Admiral's rawhide neck. "*Now*, sir." Pause. "But the Navy's not responsible for boom construction, sir. It's the Coast Guard's responsibility. According to the National Contingency Plan.

The silence in the room was electric. After a long moment Culverton said, "That's fine, sir. Thanks." His voice lost its tenseness. "And, I want another five ocean tugs and twenty tow ships. At least three thousand tons each . . . Correct, sir. We've got to erect the secondary boom in less than ten hours. What's that, sir? No, nothing else, sir. Thank you."

Culverton banged down the receiver. "Essenhigh, contact Reed. Tell him the Navy'll deliver as many boom sections as he'll need. And tell him to expect five ocean tugs and twenty tow ships. He's a free agent to set up the new boom." Culverton puckered his lips. "And Doctor, tell him to contact me immediately if there's any tomfoolery with the Navy."

Essenhigh reached for the telephone.

"What about moving the conveyor belt ships north, sir?" Matheson inquired.

"How many conveyor vessels have you got on the job?"

"Thirty-two. Wish we had more."

"There's nothing we can do about that. There are no more in service," Culverton said flatly.

Matheson picked up another phone. The Admiral looked at his watch, then across the table at Millwood.

"It'll be an hour before the next satellite picture comes in. I'm going over to the cafeteria. Coming, Captain?"

The invitation took Millwood by surprise. It clearly excluded the others.

"Cream and sugar, Captain?"

"Black, sir. Thanks."

He watched Culverton rip open a sugar package and pour the contents into a mug of steaming coffee.

"Captain," Culverton began, "after the Santa Barbara spill I was appointed to guide the President's Panel on Oil Spills. The fact that you are stewing around Dyer in frustration is connected with that panel." Culverton must have seen the puzzled look in his eyes for he added, "It's a tenuous argument, but a valid one."

Millwood was silent while Culverton cut a steak into small chunks. He appeared to be marshaling his thoughts. It wasn't until he was three-quarters of the way through the steak that he spoke again.

"*Lusitania*—Pearl Harbor—Sputnik—*Torrey Canyon*," he said suddenly, looking at Millwood, a piece of meat poised on the end of his fork. He chewed deliberately before continuing. "See the connection, Captain?"

"I get the *Lusitania* and Pearl—it took a major shock to prod America into action in both world wars. But I can't see the connection between them and the other two."

"Sputnik was another shock. Remember the times? We were boasting about the glamorous tail fins on our cars. A technological achievement! Then the Russians blasted Sputnik into orbit and caught us with our pants down!"

"And the *Torrey Canyon* was another shocker," Millwood said. "And we're still behind the eight ball."

"Exactly, Millwood. What the hell *have* we done? Tankers loaded with a quarter million tons of crude plow the high seas this minute, negotiate tricky channels, dock at ports with inches to spare. And the Japanese are building half-million tonners and designing *million* tonners, while the world sits on its ass, waiting for the next spill!"

"But I thought the President's Panel. . . . There was an official report. Essenhigh told me——"

"Gathering dust on some Washington bureaucrat's shelf," Culverton interrupted, stabbing the meat disgustedly with his fork. "If the recommendations I made in that report had been acted on, we'd have been properly organized and equipped to deal with this damned mess." He nodded toward the window. "You heard what went on just now when I called Washington. My God! All that blasted red tape for a few miles of lousy garden fencing! I could go and buy it in any hardware store if they could supply seventy miles of it."

Perhaps attending the conferences at Dye Main hadn't been wasted time after all. In the past few days Millwood had observed Culverton's executive powers in action at close quarters. He'd succeeded in mustering a clean-up fleet to fight history's biggest oil spill despite frustrating differences and uncoordinated command between surface ships, aircraft, and the government departments that controlled them. Having done that, he'd welded the opposing forces into a cohesive force. His specific job was to coordinate the scientific task force on the clean-up, but the results he'd obtained embraced more.

Culverton wiped his mouth with a napkin and settled back in the chair. The time for unburdening had arrived. "The United States has got to set up a centralized oil spill agency, on a federal level," he said deliberately. "And it's got to be part of a *world* oil spill task force. A world agency."

He waved for the steward to refill the mugs. Millwood knew he was being used as a sounding board—Culverton was waiting for signs of reaction: seeing none, the Admiral went on. "The British took a week to act before they tackled the *Torrey Canyon* spill. They didn't know the legal implications if they bombed the oil to set it on fire and burn it up. By the time they got that protocol sorted out, the oil had spread for hundreds of miles. The international legalities of spills must be ironed out. I said that in my recommendations on the President's Panel. There's nothing definite in international law on these points: Who's responsible for cleaning up? Who pays the insurance claims on damage to coastlines? How and on whom do you fix blame? Just consider claims for the cost of cleaning up—there's a whole can of worms right there! Now, with a world agency armed with legislation to act, to coordinate, maintain, and supply clean-up ships and rescue vessels —on permanent stand-by duty—we'd have a fighting chance to beat spills."

Culverton picked up his mug but put it down without drinking. "There's got to be entirely new thinking. The basic policy must be, *must* be, to prevent spills. On a worldwide basis. With new tough legislation to control tankers on the approach to harbors and docks. It takes four hours to dock a two-hundred-thousand-ton oil tanker. One poorly judged maneuver and there's a dockside spill." His eyes gleamed as the tumult of words poured out.

"What about that National Contingency Plan you mentioned on the phone, Admiral?"

"That's just weak legislation," Culverton said indignantly. "It puts the onus for cleaning up spills on state governments. The thing's too damned fragmented already. Do you know how many *federal* organizations share responsibility for cleaning spills? *Five.* There's the Federal Water Pollution Control Administration, the Geological Survey in the Department of the Interior, the Office of Emergency Planning, the Coast Guard, and even the Army Corps of Engineers. Christ, Millwood, the Army! But the Navy? Nowhere! No official responsibility! And I'm not saying that because I'm Navy." He leaned back, then forward, fingers tapping the handle of the coffee mug.

"The President's Panel urged that federal agencies have legal authority to exert control over any pollution incident. Preempt responsibility from the person or company that caused the spill. But it doesn't work like that. There have to be sharper teeth in the law." He threw his arms wide. "We're always broke! We need more money, lots of it. But the government's axed the appropriations like butchering hogs. It's only when something like this happens that Washington panics and votes through emergency funds."

Culverton shoved the mug away and leaned forward, hands gripping the table edge. "The United States government passed an oil pollution act as long ago as nineteen twenty-four," he said slowly. "When I was on the President's Panel we did some digging. No successful prosecution for pollution violations has ever been made under that act!

"There're tankers at sea this minute off United States coasts and in midocean that don't meet even the elementary safety requirements laid down by maritime law. I see you look surprised, Captain. Have you read the report of the official inquiry into the *Arrow* disaster? No? Well, I have. It's goddamned disgusting. The radar wasn't working. It hadn't worked since they loaded oil and sailed from Aruba. The depth sounder wasn't working. The gyrocompass, even that was out of service. And the standard compass. God! You'd think the captain would make certain *that* was operational. But the damned thing had a twelve-and-a-half-degree error. For most of the voyage the so-called navigator had no idea what the real error was. The only man aboard who claimed to have any idea of navigation was the captain, and there are doubts about *his* knowledge. It all came out in the inquiry, *after* two million gallons of Bunker C polluted the sea and fouled up the coast. It cost more than three million dollars for clean-up operations. And get this. They didn't even have up-to-date charts on board. All they had was one out-dated deep-sea chart. It was stamped all over in big letters: '*Not to be used in coastal waters*!'"

"Panamanian owned, wasn't she?"

"Yes. Another one of those flags of convenience things, like Liberia, Honduras, and so on. The ship was flying the Liberian flag when she was wrecked. She was under charter to Imperial Oil Limited in Canada, a subsidiary of Standard Oil of New Jersey. Everything legal. But obviously, something needs to be tightened up in international regulations controlling tanker operations."

"I'm basically a Navy man, Admiral. I don't understand the intricacies of the legalities of commercial shipping operations. Why do these tankers sail under flags of convenience?"

"Tax advantages, and ships flying Panamanian and Liberian flags can employ nonunion labor. So they pick up crews— some not well trained or safety conscious—in any port in the world and pay them the cheaper nonunion wages."

He tossed his head and smoothed back his thinning hair. "If the Navy or Coast Guard navigated ships the way some of these commercial vessels are run, we'd be a second-class naval power, Captain. I recently saw the report on the grounding of the *Vanlene* in Barkley Sound, Vancouver Island. She wasn't carrying oil, thank God. If she had we'd have had another catastrophe on our hands. It was like reading the inquiry report on the *Arrow* spill all over again. Substandard certificates of competency, virtually no navigational aids, and a captain who was forty miles north of his estimated position. Not only did he hit the wrong shore, he was even in the wrong country."

Culverton waved his arm. "Christ! And to think the pipeliners want Washington to give them the green light to build that pipeline across Alaska from Prudhoe to Valdez on the south coast and ship the crude in tankers down to the refineries near San Francisco. Right past Vancouver Island. No wonder the ecologists are alarmed. I don't blame them."

"Wasn't the *Torrey Canyon* a multination setup?" asked Millwood.

"Liberian registry. Incidentally, Liberia accounts for more than twenty per cent of the world's tanker fleet by tonnage. The *Canyon* flew the Liberian flag, was owned by Americans, chartered by Americans, and had a crew of Italians, including the captain.

"The whole setup smells. What is needed is an international agency with mandatory powers. Mandatory inspections of every tanker before she sails. Heavy penalties for offenders. Christ! You'd even have to check the compass!"

Culverton must have been bottling this up for a long time. There was obviously more to come. The Admiral pulled his chair nearer the table and drained his coffee in a series of deep gulps. He signaled the steward, who refilled his cup.

"What about you, Captain?"

Millwood pushed his cup forward silently. After the steward had left, he said, "I didn't know regulations for tankering were so haphazard."

Culverton's ideas about mandatory inspections made him uneasy. He could see the sense in making safety specifications standardized. But having inspectors come aboard at every port: his whole training and experience as a captain were against it. Culverton divined his thoughts.

"You're not one hundred percent sold on my idea, Captain," he said. "I understand. Damned hard for the man in command on the bridge to see landlubbers inspect his ship."

Millwood surprised himself by laughing.

"Airline pilots put up with it," Culverton said. "There's nobody more safety conscious than those fellows."

"So where do we go from here, sir? Your idea of a world pollution agency, I mean. To prevent spills at sea."

Culverton made a hopeless gesture. "Some of the countries brought it up at the United Nations Conference on the Human Environment at Stockholm. Sure, everybody voted for it. Like motherhood. But nothing was decided. It'll be years before we get something practical that works on an international scale. Too many vested interests involved. The oil companies, maritime insurance brokers, shipbuilders, demand for automobiles and more gas to drive them. More demand for oil to help solve the energy crisis."

"You said the United Nations should take over, sir."

Culverton's eyes gleamed. "Here's a chance for that inept organization to come to grips with a problem that affects everybody. It would have the blessing of every yachtsman off Long Island whose hull is fouled by bilge oil discharged from ships, every fisherman on the Grand Banks, every swimmer who has to scrape tar off his feet on Malibu Beach—and Atlantic City and Miami Beach and Torremolinos and Capetown. The oil companies would benefit. Do you think Standard Oil or Shell or Gulf like losing oil at sea? There's the financial loss, the lousy publicity, the hue and cry of the conservationists. Plus the money they pay out for cleaning up. The oil companies that do try to prevent oil spills would benefit tremendously if an international safety agency got down to the nitty-gritty. Have you seen this?" He fished a folded newspaper clipping from his pocket, unfolded it, and read:

" 'American Cyanamid Company, Georgia, has made an official request to the United States Army Corps of Engineers to dump one million gallons of sulphuric acid and toxic metals every four days into the Gulf Stream. The company would, if granted permission, barge the acid to a point eighty-seven miles off the Georgia coast and dump it into the Gulf Stream. The company claims the dilution by the sea water will render the waste practically harmless.' "

The Admiral looked up. "The world's plain crazy, Captain." He flicked the paper with his fingertips. "Seven industrial companies are lurking in the wings waiting for the Washington verdict. My God! Using the ocean as an industrial garbage dump!"

Culverton carefully folded the paper and tucked it in his pocket. After a silence Millwood asked, "What happened after you made your report to the President's Panel, sir?"

"Nothing. Nothing at all. But it's not all black. I must be fair. I was particularly impressed with the studies by the Intergovernmental Maritime Consultative Organization. They've been looking at ideas on shipping of all hazardous materials, not just petroleum products. And they're also looking at navigation safety and even ship design. The Department of Transport in Washington is studying these things too, but there are still no adequate controls for the design, manning, operation, regulation, inspection, and legal liabilities of oil tankers on the high seas, on coastal waters subject to international jurisdiction, and on canals and other inland waterways."

Millwood wondered why a man like Culverton had never gone into politics. He'd make a fine senator. On reflection, he decided Culverton, a man of action all his life, would be stultified by the slow grind of the Washington processes. He knew from the experience of several of his friends, that bureaucratic drag drove some of the best American brains into limbo. There must be hundreds of Naval and Coast Guard officers—and businessmen running their own affairs—who took early retirement and went deep-sea cruising or cultivated roses or settled into obscure California ranchhouses to write their memoirs. The Admiral's voice broke into his thoughts.

"I couldn't drive this point home to those bureaucrats in Washington, Captain. Under existing international law no nation can interfere with a ship at sea, even though it may be in danger of releasing huge quantities of oil into the ocean. They can't even interfere with normal salvage operations, even if they want to help minimize pollution hazards. You saw the hassling that went on with those Canadian government fellows when they worried over whether *North Star* had sunk in Canadian territorial waters. You know that under international law a nation has to wait until a vessel in distress enters its territorial waters before that country can take over direction of the vessel—"

He broke off as urgent footsteps clattered on the tiled corridor outside. Essenhigh burst through the door and looked around frantically, sweat beading his pink cheeks.

"Admiral!" the tubby man shouted breathlessly. "The boom's burst!"

TEN

"It couldn't stand the pressure. Dragged out a half-mile section," Meschino explained as Millwood dashed into the room.

Culverton grabbed the telephone from Meschino. "Who's on the line?" he demanded.

"Reed, sir," Meschino said.

"Captain Reed! What happened? . . . No reserve sections? Grab them from the second boom! You've got to plug that hole!"

Culverton looked up at the ceiling, his face distorted. He looked at Essenhigh. "The oil's taken out your second boom before they got it into position! The center of the boom's a gonner!" He listened again, and said into the receiver, "Oil two miles past the breach, Captain? I'll get peat moss dropped right away. Stand by. I'll be back to you!"

Culverton stabbed the button on the telephone. "Chief of Air Services! Top priority call!" He replaced the telephone. It immediately rang imperiously, echoing in the lofty room. "Muster all the peat moss you've got, General. The center of the boom's washed out. I want an airdrop to cover the complete gap beginning at—Hold on a moment." He clapped his hand over the mouthpiece. "Essenhigh, get that latest satellite map from General Newton. Read off the position of the boom at the halfway mark."

Essenhigh scrambled to unroll the map. He read off the numerals. The Admiral repeated them over the telephone. Essenhigh had drawn a circle around the center of the thin red line that indicated the boom and the air curtain, a line that stretched across the center of Davis Strait between Greenland on one side and the Labrador coast on the other. The main thrust of the spill would be at this point. Millwood tried to shove aside a horrible thought, but it persisted—once the oil was snapped up by the Labrador Current, it would be carried south around Newfoundland and Nova Scotia, along the Maine and Massachusetts coasts—as far as Cape Cod.

"Get Reed again," the Admiral commanded. General Newton rushed to the door as an officer stepped in with a new satellite map. Newton fumbled with some heavy glass ashtrays, trying to hold down the curled edges of the map as he unrolled it on the table. He upset a tray, scattering cigarette butts and ashes over the map. A Coast Guard lieutenant smartly stepped forward, tore a sheet of paper from a scrap pad, and neatly scooped up the offending material.

"Captain Reed, I've ordered an air drop of peat moss to cover the breach. That'll slow it down and relieve the pressure. In the meantime, I'm going to order the end-of-the-boom ships to move the last five miles of their sections toward you. In case the breach widens. They can plug the gap with the moss for the time being—I hope."

The door burst open and an Air Force officer with a radio insignia on his sleeve rushed past Millwood. "Sir! Admiral," he shouted, "there's an urgent message! From the lead patrol plane, sir. Take it on Line Four!"

Without hesitation Culverton calmly pressed a button.

"Ready to receive message, lead patrol plane," he said into the telephone.

Millwood glanced around the room. Every face was fixed on the Admiral's.

"The whole boom's going! What the hell are the ships doing? Aren't they on station where they're supposed to be?" The room fell silent again. "Lieutenant, fly the whole length again and report back!"

Culverton let the telephone hang limply at the end of his arm. He turned to the others. "The whole damned thing's gone—a complete washout all along the line! The patrol plane reports it looks like a bunch of broken matchsticks."

"Jesus Christ!" Millwood heard Meschino whisper in an awed voice. "Forty million gallons!"

Your bugs won't do any good now, he thought without malice. Nor the air bubbles and dispersal chemicals. Maybe the peat moss, lumpy with congealing oil, could be netted by trawlers and towed ashore. That would be something. But the huge spill would soon cover thousands of square miles. Nothing would stop it now. It would gather momentum as it got caught in the measured creep of the icy seas, streaming inexorably southward toward the warmer waters of the Atlantic and the Gulf Stream's westward sweep. At this moment, the oil rolling over the ocean surface must already be upsetting the delicate air-water interface temperature. Soon the dark waters would absorb the sun's heat and transfer it below the surface, upsetting the life of the plankton, interfering with their nightly ascent to the surface to feed and daily descent. Fish depended on plankton for food. Millwood wished he knew more about marine biology, so that he could understand more of what was in store when the oil smothered the seas in the southern latitudes. These scientists and their ideas had failed. Even the practical boom had failed. Unless somebody came up with a revolutionary idea, something entirely new—and quickly—the oil was going to keep rolling south.

Millwood awoke. The sun was shining brilliantly through the window of the hut. He looked at his watch: 08:00. Damn, he'd overslept. The last three days at Dye Main had been days of unbearable frustration. Meschino and Essenhigh and the others had flown over the spill as far south as Cape Race, and Admiral Culverton had inspected the westerly flow of oil past the Nova Scotia coast. Radio warnings as far south as Portland, Maine, had instructed fishing boats and shrimpers to haul in nets and make for port. As he dressed hurriedly, other events of the past days coursed through his mind. The signals flashed from ships on the Grand Banks as the advancing edge of oil swirled out of the fog, enveloping dories and fouling their nets. A Russian factory ship, lagging behind to catch more fish despite the radio warnings to clear off, had reported the loss of its entire day's catch. The skipper threatened legal action against the Prudhoe-Northwest Passage Corporation.

A knock came at the door. He stuffed his shirt into his pants. It was a Coast Guard lieutenant. "Morning, Captain. You're going in Admiral Culverton's plane, sir, to Boston. He's transferring his base of operations there."

"Boston?" He could tell from the look on the lieutenant's face what was coming.

"Yes, Captain. There's a rumor they're closing the harbor." He checked his watch. "Forty-five minutes, sir? That'll give you time for a quick breakfast."

"Thanks, Lieutenant."

The spill would have lost momentum by the time it got as far south as Boston. Did Culverton intend to construct a boom around Boston Harbor? A boom might stand the lessened pressure there. And the oil would be thinned out.

He quickly washed and shaved, threw his few possessions into a small duffle bag, and went to the cafeteria. Opening the door, he saw Essenhigh and Meschino seated at a table. Meschino pointed to a chair.

"Morning, Captain."

"Morning. What's the news?"

Essenhigh stuck out his fat lower lip but said nothing.

"How bad is it? I overslept."

"You've heard about the Grand Banks, I guess?" Essenhigh asked. He had bags under his eyes and his cheeks were pale.

"It's well into the coastal regions west of the Banks," Meschino said, sinking his teeth into a piece of buttered toast. "It's been seen by observers on the cliffs off the south coast of Nova Scotia. There's a southwesterly arm curling down towards Maine. Coffee?"

It seemed dreamlike. These scientists were talking as if they were verbalizing a technical report. Especially Meschino. He was young, enthusiastic, ambitious. He'd been treating this like some sort of exercise, some practical treatise that would get him promotion. He talked almost with relish of the spill curling around the Maine coast. Idiot. Millwood wondered whether Sable Island, south of Nova Scotia, was in the spill's path. That would be ironic. An oil company had an offshore drilling rig off Sable's sandy shore. Conservationists had played hell when the company had proposed the idea. For years there had been wild horses on the island, believed to be the offspring of animals that had swum ashore from wrecked sailing ships. The drillers would pollute the island and harm the horses, conservationists claimed. But the horses had survived, although the Ipswich Sparrow, a tiny bird that bred only on Sable Island, had not. So few had been seen in the last few years that naturalists had placed the bird on the official endangered-species list.

"What's going to happen when you fellows get to Boston?" Millwood asked.

"The Admiral's got a bee in his bonnet it'll be easier to coordinate the scientific groups and the operational groups from Boston," Meschino said.

"It makes sense," said Essenhigh. "We're out of the picture up here."

Culverton was nobody's fool, Millwood reflected. In Boston he'd be in a strong position to organize both Coast Guard and Navy ships, plus the other clean-up forces he'd need—and perhaps more important, he could reach the public from Boston.

Essenhigh looked up. "Here's the Admiral now," he said, sitting back. Millwood rose: Meschino made a feeble attempt to raise his bottom from his seat.

"Morning, Captain," Culverton said. He seemed preoccupied and merely nodded at the others.

"Good morning, Admiral," Millwood replied.

"Where're Matheson and the others?" Culverton demanded.

"He was in the radio shack about a half hour ago, sir. Everybody was listening to the New York broadcast."

"Scaring the populace again," Culverton grunted.

"There ought to be a law," Meschino said. "There's another satellite map on the way, sir. Are you going to wait for it before taking off?"

Culverton glanced at his watch. "Give it ten minutes. If it doesn't arrive by then, get Matheson to have a copy delivered immediately to Boston Coast Guard base. Is that clear?"

"Yes, Admiral."

Millwood strained to see below, anxious for his first look at Boston since he'd put to sea in *North Star*. It seemed years since he'd left the dock on a sunny day only three weeks earlier, listening to the cheers from the workers who had seen them off. Herbert Armstrong and the other company brass had waved from the little platform that had been erected for the sailing ceremony. He could still hear Simoncelli's cheery "so long!" booming across the widening gap as the submarine moved from dockside.

Conversation between the Admiral and the others had long since subsided. Fifteen minutes after leaving Cape Dyer they'd run into cloud and the pilot had climbed. When the clouds finally parted, he caught a glimpse of cliffs with a lighthouse. Marblehead Light. Quickly he oriented himself. A causeway came into view. They were over Marblehead Neck. To port, buried in the murk, was the vague form of Tinkers Island. They'd be about twelve miles from Logan International Airport, he estimated.

"A message for you, Admiral," the pilot called. He handed a set of headphones to Culverton and plugged a trailing cable into a socket on the dashboard. Culverton pulled on the headset.

"Fine," Millwood heard him say. "Get a direct link-up with Washington. Anything from Houston yet on the weather map?"

The pilot opened the throttle, drowning out the one-sided conversation. The assembling headquarters staff at Boston would be making frantic arrangements to deal with the spill. Sunshine flooded the cabin. Several Coast Guard officers and junior scientists from Matheson's team turned simultaneously to look out of the windows.

Culverton yanked off the headset and turned to Essenhigh. "We're setting up headquarters at the Naval Yard in Charlestown," he said. "The Navy's laying on a special communications setup."

"Good," Essenhigh said.

"The latest weather map's negative. Ten-ten cloud over eastern Newfie and southern Nova Scotia. As soon as we land, get the reports from the choppers flying up the coast."

Essenhigh nodded. The layer of thin cloud dissipated, and Millwood studied the seascape. East Point skimmed below. They were over Massachusetts Bay. Several ships slipped by, inward bound, followed by a fleet of fishing boats, probably the Boston fleet. Funny to see them headed toward land this time of day. Deer Island slid below the fuselage. They were off course for Logan, if that was their destination. He glanced at the pilot, who moved his head from side to side, scanning the sky ahead. The machine turned, lost height, and they were over land. Millwood recognized the finger docks of the Naval Reservation, and there was the city in the distance, the golden dome of the State House on Beacon Hill glinting in the sunlight. They slid over the inner harbor, and he saw airplanes parked around the southwest terminal at Logan. The plane slowed, turned, and descended. In a moment a damp runway appeared outside the window. A jouncing bump told him they had landed.

Culverton looked grimly around the huge conference room. "Our options, gentlemen, are few. I'm not going to go into the woefully inadequate measures we've taken and the lack of coordination. Prevention has failed; containment has failed. Unless by some fortunate discovery at this late hour somebody comes up with a new method or process to clean up the oil, we're left with the conventional mechanical booms, air bubble curtains, dispersants, sinking agents, and the rest. You're all familiar with them."

He paused and looked at several men in the front row. "We are fortunate in having with us several authorities and specialists on oil clean-up from Germany, France, and Britain. Many met these distinguished gentlemen late last night at our first hasty get-together. The governments of the countries represented have promised to supply equipment, materials, ships, and help in clean-up operations. I also understand that——"

Culverton looked up as the technician at the big screen whispered in his ear. "Here comes the first output," he announced, swiveling his chair to face the screen. The technician pushed a button on the console. A big screen against the far wall suddenly became alive, flickered with light that stabilized into a soft green background. The room lights went out, and Millwood watched the diagrammatic outline of the east coast from Cape Cod north to New Brunswick take shape. Computer characters and numbers appeared at the top righthand corner of the screen. "Terminal now active," he read. The room was hushed, expectant.

"Code: Mass Spill. Time: Zero-seven-three-three," said a flat mechanical voice from remote speakers. "Synoptic report follows. Oil on the surface is ponding in a forty-square-mile area between Portland, Maine, and Cape St. Mary, Nova Scotia, at a point fifteen miles from the coast. The oil has an anticyclonic circulation with offshoots estimated to be one mile broad curving in a southwesterly direction at an estimated four knots. The oil at this point is firmly in the grip of the coastwise stream of the Labrador Current. Observers at Portland report that the spill can be observed from shore. Coastwise traffic has been advised to return to port. Fish canning and preservation plants in Portland processing fish caught in Casco Bay are being inspected by biologists from the Food and Drug Administration, Washington. Sales of fish have been temporarily banned by government order."

Several officers near Millwood gasped audibly.

"The freighter *India Reknown*, one hundred miles off Halifax, heading for Savannah, Georgia, reported fifteen minutes ago she was completely surrounded by oil. She is sailing a south-southwesterly course. Her master, Captain Hamid, measured the oil with a probe and reports it was two inches thick. Vessel's speed has been reduced. Captain Hamid has been instructed to take probes every sea mile and report to Houston. He has been instructed to radio immediately when his vessel clears the oil.

"Helicopters continuing patrol of the Grand Banks report several square miles of sea covered with dead fish. A heavy fog over the eastern Banks has forced Air Command to call off the air patrol in that area. Sea is calm; oil is now fully ponded with zero—repeat zero—movement.

"Fixed wing aircraft from Dye Main patrolling northern Davis Strait, at site of *North Star*'s sinking, report crude streaming to the surface. Surface conditions in the area rapidly deteriorating as high pressure ridge over Greenland west coast gives way to depression centered over North Atlantic. Farther south, in the lower Strait, Canadian government sources report extensive oil pollution on coastal region south of latitude sixty from Cape Uivak. The bodies of several thousand seabirds have been sighted on the rocks and offshore ice fields in the area south of Deep Inlet. Aircraft dispatched from Goose Bay report hundreds of dead seals on the ice and floating carcasses in the inlets in the Gulf of St. Lawrence. The transatlantic liner *Queen Elizabeth Two*, outward bound from Southampton, reports meeting a slick of crude oil when crossing longitude thirty degrees twenty-seven minutes and eleven seconds west."

Somebody at the head table rustled a chart. A vague form got up, partly obscuring the screen as the chart was handed to the Admiral. The screen dimmed and brightened, a switch clicked, and Millwood was staring at an electronic diagram outlining the mid-Atlantic region. The Newfoundland east coast was on the extreme lefthand side, and the southern tip of Greenland and the whole of Iceland toward the top. To the far right Ireland and Land's End stood out as well-defined shapes. A curved longitude line flashed on the screen, with the numeral 30. That far east! In the North Atlantic Current.

"The *Queen Elizabeth Two* reports a continuous band of oil approximately three hundred yards wide. Course has twice been altered to avoid the slick, but there now appear to be several hundred separate slicks in the process of joining. All smoking on board has been forbidden, including below decks, and shipping in the region has been warned . . . warned . . ."

Heads jerked as the voice faltered.

A click, followed by a loud *plip.* "A radio report from Hamilton, Bermuda. A slick extending in a west-to-east direction is lying off approximately ten miles to the north of the island. Estimates of the length of the slick vary between nineteen and twenty-seven miles. The Governor, on behalf of the British Government, has registered an official warning of liability to the United States Government in the event the slick is washed ashore. The warning has been given, the Governor explained, after due consultation with Whitehall, on the grounds that submarine tanker *North Star* is of United States registry and was under the command of a United States national. . . ."

"Idiotic politicians!" Essenhigh muttered in a stage whisper.

"Oceanographers from the Scripps Institution of Oceanography are now taking precise measurements of tide levels at Portugal Cove, Newfoundland, Portland, Boston, and New York harbors. Preliminary reports from Portugal Cove indicate higher than normal levels are due to large inflows of water. Although not confirmed, scientists believe that heat absorption by the oil now covering several thousand square miles of ocean is responsible for the rapid melting of offshore ice fields in various Baffin Bay and Davis Strait localities. This is the end of first report Code: Mass Spill."

Bodies relaxed, then stiffened as the voice blurted, "Lateflash, lateflash. Code: Mass Spill. Lobster traps pulled up at Yarmouth, Maine, and Gloucester, Massachusetts, contain dead lobsters. Biologists have examined the lobsters and report crude oil penetrating their shells. No oil—repeat, no oil—has been observed on the surface of the sea at Gloucester or within one hundred miles north of the area. The nearest surface oil is in the ponding area off Portland, Maine. Fishery officials at Gloucester, in conjunction with officials from the local department of public health, have issued warnings against eating lobsters and all other shellfish pending investigation by the Food and Drug Administration."

The screen now showed a huge blowup of the great sweep of the coast between Cape Cod and Bar Harbor, Maine, and beyond.

"One theory is that ponding oil off Portland, subject to submarine currents, is being emulsified and carried beneath the surface in a southerly direction. As a result, all clam, oyster, scallop, crab, lobster, and shrimp fishing along the Maine and Massachusetts coasts has been banned by the Federal Government. Notices to this effect have been issued to all fishing industries and the public has been warned by radio and television messages and other media. Scientists from the Massachusetts Audubon Society are patrolling the north shore of Cape Cod from Provincetown to Plymouth Bay Lighthouse to examine marine life offshore. Samples are being sent to the United States Bureau of Fisheries at the Woods Hole Oceanographic Institution for biological examination. All fishing in the Cape Cod area has been terminated. The Provincetown fishing fleet is returning to harbor. The Boston fleets, both the inshore and Grand Banks fleets, have been ordered to remain in harbor. Several Boston trawlers have reported nets ruined by oil on the Grand Banks. This is the end of first report Code: Mass Spill."

The screen dimmed and blacked out. The room lights came on. The atmosphere was stifling. Millwood took a deep breath and turned to Essenhigh.

"What now, Doctor?"

"The Admiral said he wanted think-tanks organized. In the hope some fresh ideas develop. You could sit in."

"Me? Are you kidding? I'm a sailor, not a scientist."

"Stay anyway, Captain. You'll find it interesting."

"All right, I'll stay," growled Millwood. "But I need some chow first. I'm going to the mess."

ELEVEN

Millwood stepped outside the gate of the Naval Reservation. The sentry on duty saluted smartly. The weather had cleared. Bright sunlight filled the dock area. To the left he saw the superstructure of a cruiser in the drydock, a crew of electronic technicians swarming over the dish-and-rod antennas high above deck. Farther out was the glint of water, and in the distance several trawlers bucking a strong headwind as they plowed past Deer Island Lighthouse.

"Taxi, Captain?"

He swung around. The young Navy ensign had red hair and a freckled face, and saluted with exaggerated correctness. Millwood looked at the waiting line of taxis and private cars.

"No, thanks. I'll walk a little way."

The ensign looked disappointed. Millwood strode down Harbor Street, his head low, and crossed the railway tracks. After the Mass Spill report the meeting had broken up into groups according to scientific disciplines, preparatory to forming teams. Essenhigh had surrounded himself with about ten physicists. Meschino had taken several experts in tow and led them into a room adjoining the big hall. Matheson and Admiral Culverton had collected two dozen younger men, and the last vision he'd had of the group was of Matheson preparing to lecture them like a university professor. Millwood had left, despite his reluctant promise to Essenhigh to stay.

In a few moments he had reached the corner. Perhaps he should have taken the ensign's offer after all: the few taxis that rushed past were occupied, and it was a good mile to the bridge at Fort Point Channel. He turned right and set off. Several staff cars emerged from the Naval Annex across the road, and he caught a glimpse of gold shoulder braid and peaked caps as the limousines sped toward the city. There was a sudden swish of tires as a car braked beside him at the curb. A horn blared, and a familiar face smiled at him through an open window.

"May I give you a lift, Captain?"

Millwood stared. It was Eva. He grabbed the door handle and jumped into the car. Millwood felt the seat thump his back as she pressed the accelerator, and was conscious of the faint odor of perfume.

"I just left the shipyard, Captain. What were you doing? *Walking* into town?"

"I intended to go part way. My car's stuck at a service station having a tune-up. I'm a fish out of water back there." He nodded toward the Yard.

"I wondered how you'd make out when I heard you were official observer for the company. Is it really bad, Captain?"

He sidestepped the question. "What are you doing now?" he asked.

"Me? Oh, I'm back in the Navy's electronics lab," she said brightly. She flashed a look at him. "Everybody's worried

175

about the ponding off Portland and scared of what it might do to Boston and the Cape. There're wild rumors flying about."

"Such as?" he demanded.

"About the oil getting caught in a submarine current and reappearing off the coast here. Is it possible, Captain?"

"Yes. Keep it to yourself, Eva. You understand?"

"Of course," she said. "What's going to happen now? About cleaning up the mess?"

"They're splitting up into teams. There's a crew of physicists working on some ideas, a group of chemical experts, and Culverton—he's the Admiral in charge of coordinating the whole scientific team—is talking coastal clean-up with a bunch of ecologists. There's been some serious damage up the northern coast. As bad as Kivitooluk. You've heard, I suppose?"

She nodded. "Where shall I drop you off?"

He had a sudden disappointed feeling. "Oh, any place where it's convenient. I live over in Woburn. I can get a taxi in town."

"I'm going that way, Captain." She swerved to avoid a car that veered into her lane. "It's people like that that make me itch to be back at sea."

Millwood smiled. "You sound ready to weigh anchor, Eva."

"What happened to Mr. Simoncelli," Eva asked.

"Back in Texas. He flew up in his helicopter day before yesterday. I heard he's trying to sort out the insurance problems on *North Star*."

Eva turned up a ramp leading to the expressway. "Wonder if there's anything new on the radio?" She leaned forward and pressed a button.

". . . while at the same time there's an unconfirmed report that crude oil has been sighted about fifteen miles off Boston.

Scientists at the coordination center at the Navy Shipyard Headquarters refuse to comment. However, our traffic helicopter reporter Robert Blakeley has been moved from his regular job reporting traffic conditions on Route one-twenty-eight and is now over Massachusetts Bay. Come in Robert Blakeley!"

The radio crackled. Millwood glanced at Eva. She stared ahead, her mouth strained and puckered.

"This . . . Blakeley . . . now. . . ."

Eva's hand darted forward and turned up the volume. She twiddled the tuning knob. ". . . over Massachusetts Bay approaching Boston Harbor. I'm about twenty miles out, directly east of Logan International, at one thousand feet, passing over a calm sea entirely empty of shipping. It's a strange sight, this empty sea. The approaches here are usually crowded with ships and fishing boats this time of day. The only craft I can see is a small sailboat making it down to the Cape. There's no trace of oil. Bert Tunny, our dockside reporter, heard a story that oil's been sighted in Massachusetts Bay. I'm going down to five hundred feet if I can get clearance from Logan. Stand by while I contact Logan control. . . ."

The radio buzzed. Culverton would have a fleet of patrol vessels in the Bay if oil had showed up on the satellite picture, Millwood thought. A thing like that wouldn't get past *him*. Besides, it was about two hundred miles from the ponding off Portland to Massachusetts Bay. It seemed impossible for oil to be caught in an underwater current and transported that distance.

The radio crackled. "I'm descending to five hundred feet," the voice boomed. "The rollers out here are medium high. I'm going slower now. About twelve miles out. There's more seaweed and floating garbage than usual—maybe the way the wind's blowing. That sailboat looks like she's going all out for the Cape. She's gone about. On the other tack now. Let's go over and have a look at her. She's not too far away. Over to the left—to port as sailors say." Eva and Millwood exchanged disgusted glances. "There's a man and a woman on board. They're getting along nicely, fair wind on the sea. But their boat is plowing through something that looks like black cream—it's oil! Curling up across the bow. The hull is black up to the deck as she leans to the wind. There's a pool of oil around them, the sun glistening on it as I come around the other side. It goes in a great crescent, pointing toward the land. I'm over the end of it now, away from the sailboat. There's another slick, about a half mile farther on! And another! The whole Bay's full of them!"

Millwood and Eva looked at each other again. It *was* true then. It would only be a matter of time now. Unless they got rid of the oil swirling in a slow massive movement off the Maine coast, tons of it would appear off Boston.

His mind flashed back to the conference. He looked at his watch.

"I'd better tell them back there," he said. "They may not know about it."

"Surely they'd pick up this broadcast," Eva protested.

"They're tuned to their own communications system. Everything's computerized, with NASA Space Center in Houston coordinating all incoming intelligence. There's no way of knowing if there's somebody listening to this fellow in his chopper. He's on a local broadcast wave band. I'm going to call Admiral Culverton."

"You can phone from my place. It's not far from here."

"I can see streaks of oil farther south now, heading along the coast toward Plymouth. There's a long line of oil, about two or three hundred yards long, behind the breakers rolling in toward Nantasket Beach way down to Cohasset. There's going to be a huge clean-up job if that stuff gets ashore."

A voice cut into Blakeley's. "This is Bert Tunny again. While Robert Blakeley is going down to the Cape, here's an earlier taped report from an eyewitness over the Grand Banks fishing grounds. As listeners to our earlier report know, the Boston fishing fleet has returned from the Grand Banks and is now safely tied up in harbor. Here's that report from CBS News."

"The fog lifted about noon and a pale sun is now shining down on the waters of the Banks. To the west I can see the last of the Boston fishing boats as they make tracks for home, with here and there a straggler trying to catch up. Farther south are several bigger ships, Russian factory and canning vessels, mixed in with some Japanese and Spanish trawlers. For the first time in probably hundreds of years the famous Grand Banks are nearly deserted. This plane I'm in is now wheeling slowly over a calm sea, a copper-colored sea wearing a layer of golden black oil——"

"What's he think he is?" Millwood muttered. "A poet?"

"——like a crown of anguish. As we bank I can see millions of dead fish floating belly up in the swell flattened under the weight of the mantle of oil. We're climbing now. Three thousand feet, four, leveling off at five thousand. All I can see in every direction is oil, floating on a dull——"

"We get the picture!" Eva snapped, flicking off the radio. In a few minutes the car stopped in front of a small bungalow in a pleasant tree-lined street.

"Here we are," Eva said. Millwood followed her through the front door. "The phone's in the front room," she said. "I'll put on some coffee."

Millwood flipped the pages of the telephone book and found the Navy Yard number. While he waited to be connected with Culverton he looked around the room. It had a pleasant lived-in feeling despite Eva's frequent absences at sea. Near the telephone table was a bookcase that looked as though it was in constant use: the jackets on the electronics textbooks had been repaired with transparent tape. Several volumes on navigation were piled haphazardly on the top shelf. A printed wiring circuit board fashioned in the form of a submarine stood on the buffet, with an electric clock set in the miniature sail. The room had warmth. He glanced at the pictures on the far wall expectantly. But there were no family pictures, only small reproductions of famous ships: *Old Ironsides*, *Cutty Sark*, and an engraving of the raising of the ancient Swedish warship *Wasa*. The telephone buzzed and clicked.

"Culverton here," announced a familiar voice.

"It's Captain Millwood, sir. There's a radio report on a local station that oil's been sighted in the Bay."

"It came over the monitor a few minutes ago, Captain. Thank you." There was a pause. "I haven't had a chance to talk to you since we got this coordinating conference going. Where are you now?"

"At a friend's house, uptown."

"You'll be coming back? These sessions should be over before the next report's due."

Millwood hesitated. "Of course, sir."

"I understand your feelings, Captain." Culverton's voice carried a sympathetic inflection. "But if you stay on the inside you'll be better briefed for the public inquiry."

"Public inquiry, sir?" Millwood's throat went dry.

"Washington's arranging it. Playing up to public reaction about the spill. With an election coming up, the politicians are jittery. Better get back here, Captain. The next report's due in thirty-eight minutes."

Before Millwood had a chance to reply, there was a click. A sudden depression swept over him. He'd have to give evidence in public on how he'd lost *North Star*. Culverton was trying to make the going easier for him. Maybe he'd lost a ship during his career and gone through the repetitive nightmare of reliving those dreadful minutes leading to the moment he'd ordered, "Abandon ship!"

The clattering of dishes in the kitchen broke into his thoughts. Eva appeared in the doorway.

"Black as usual, Captain?" she asked.

Millwood shook himself. "Thanks, Eva. By the way, you can drop that 'Captain' stuff. At least in your own home!"

Her eyes twinkled. It was hard to believe that the attractive woman standing in the doorway balancing the silver tray with the coffee things was the same electronics engineer who had worked alongside him in *North Star*'s control room, the expert who had rectified the fault in the bum electronic sonar gear.

"Sorry they're not man-size mugs like the ones we had on *North Star*, Frank." She handed him a cup filled to the brim. Millwood nodded at the picture of the *Wasa*.

"That was some salvage operation," he said.

"You've heard about it?"

"I've seen it. In that special museum in Stockholm where they automatically spray it with liquid plastic every hour to preserve the wood."

Eva's face lit up with pleasure. "You're the first person I've met in America who's even heard of it, Frank!"

"Covered in silt for a couple hundred years, if I remember," he said. Glumly he added, "It would be different with *North Star*. We've seen the last of her, I'm afraid." He was conscious of an awkward silence.

"You punish yourself too much, Frank."

He put down the cup and looked at her. She was sitting in the armchair opposite, her saucer on her knee. He saw the cool gray eyes. They held neither sympathy nor criticism.

"My father was a seadog of the old school, and so was my

grandfather. Father cuffed my ears every time I made a mistake. It gets into the psyche after so many years. I'm too old now to shake it off. The guilt feeling, I mean." He paused and added, "It's not until a man gets to fifty that he really knows what makes him tick. Understands why he does things a certain way and why he feels the things he does."

He broke off abruptly. An old inhibition clamped down: a reluctance to talk freely about his personal feelings to members of his crew. As an executive officer, he knew well the famous loneliness of command. He glanced at Eva. She was looking at him expectantly. "Anyway, what's done, is done," he said offhandedly, and looked down at his cup.

"Who're you trying to convince, Frank? Yourself or me?"

His head snapped up. "Eva, for God's sake don't tell me I'm punishing myself for nothing! In the final analysis I'm a skipper who lost his ship. A very special kind of ship. A ship that set out to prove something—and failed—because *I* rammed her into an iceberg."

"There was thick fog when you surfaced—and besides, the leak had already begun days before. And the surface radar was unreliable. You can't blame yourself for everything." The cup rattled as she put it down.

"I know, I know," he said in a tired voice. "I've been over it a million times. But hell—in peacetime, in a calm sea?"

"What will happen now that there's oil in the Bay?" she asked, obviously changing the subject.

Millwood shrugged. "Bring down some of the conveyor belt ships and probably build a floating boom around the slick. I don't know," he said hopelessly. "I wish they'd get somebody else to attend as official company observer besides the company big brass. I'm sick of it."

He saw her flash him a covert glance. "I understand how

you feel, Frank. It's like being on trial. But you're the only person qualified for the job."

"There's going to be a public inquiry, Eva. I'll be called to give evidence. We'll all have to attend, at least the crew will have to be present for part of the time if they're called upon to give evidence."

"Public inquiry? Who said?"

"Admiral Culverton—he just told me." He nodded at the telephone on the side table. "The politicians are making a circus of it. Cashing in on public reaction."

She fell silent. "I don't think a public inquiry is like a court, is it?" she asked dubiously after a moment of reflection.

"Search me. I have an idea it might be worse. I'll have to give an account of the factors leading up to the loss of *North Star*."

There was a pause.

"I've got to be going." He looked at his watch. "The next report on the spill is due in twenty minutes. I'll have to pick up my car some other time. I've got to get back to the Naval Reservation. I'll call a taxi."

She got up. "I need some fresh air, Frank." Her voice was determined. "The least I can do is drive my old skipper back to town."

"Thanks, Eva," he said, wishing he didn't have to go. He stood a moment looking down into her face, conscious of a silent sigh escaping him.

"You have a button missing," she said, touching the sagging lapel of his jacket. "Have you got it? I'll sew it on."

Millwood grunted. "Yes, I put it in my pocket, I think. Before we left *North Star*." He fumbled in his pocket. "But don't bother. I'll fix it later. There's no time."

"It won't take a minute. I've met Navy officers before who

promised to sew on lost buttons. They never do. Slip it off, Frank. I'll get a needle and thread." She disappeared into the kitchen.

He took off his jacket and restraightened his tie. Eva reappeared and took the jacket from him. He couldn't believe a button could be sewn on so quickly. In a minute Eva handed the jacket to him. "Thank you. All it needs now is a dry cleaning and it'll be good as new."

She laughed and put the needle and thread on the mantel. For a long moment she hesitated, studying his face.

"Shall we go?" she said at last.

TWELVE

". . . studied all your reports," Culverton was saying as Millwood opened the door at the back of the crowded hall. He silently shut it behind him. A Coast Guard lieutenant, spotting his captain's stripes, rose from a seat at the end of the back aisle. Millwood raised his hand. "Thanks, I'll stand," he whispered, finding himself a spot against the wall.

"Some schemes are ingenious," the Admiral continued, "but none of them deal with a method of stopping, or even slowing, the oil flow from the north." He strode to a large map of Baffin Bay and Davis Strait.

"There, and here!" he said, tapping the tip of a pointer on the map. "That's where our whole problem lies. Stop it here, and we can deal with the shore clean-up."

He threw the pointer down on the table and looked at the scattered maps and papers. "This idea of a burn-off off Portland," he said, thumping a pad of papers and shaking his head. "Useless unless we stop it up in Davis Strait. And I question the advisability and effectiveness of a burn-off. We may light a bonfire that will continually be refueled as the oil drifts down from Nova Scotia. We must cut it off up north!"

RAGE UNDER THE ARCTIC

Millwood glanced at his watch. The video report was due in less than two minutes. He wondered how far the oil had swung down toward the Cape. Perhaps Culverton had started to build a boom north of Boston and even moved conveyor-belt ships into position. He had a vision of the crude oil creeping past Castel Park promontory, gathering speed and sweeping past the wharves at the mouth of the Mystic River.

"The Coast Guard's assembling a boom outside the entrance to Boston Harbor," Culverton said. "Conveyor-belt ships are standing by. The report on the ponding off Maine is bad." He picked up a ribbon of teletype paper and ran his eye down the column. "This interim report just came in. As fast as the conveyor-belt ships lap up the oil, it's replenished from the westward flow farther up the coast."

A lieutenant stepped forward and whispered to him. "The latest report's ready," the Admiral said. The room darkened. A green light flickered on the screen, stabilized, and brightened. But to Millwood's surprise, instead of a map of the eastern United States seaboard, an outline of the British Isles and the wide sweep of the Norwegian coast appeared, with Ireland and the intervening seas.

"Code: Mass Spill," announced the mechanical voice. "Time: sixteen-three-one. A Danish fishing vessel returning to Tórshavn in the Faeroe Islands, four hundred miles north of Scotland, reports sailing through seas covered with blobs of congealed oil and tar. Measurements of sample blobs follow: four and one quarter inches diameter, two and one half inches diameter, and one inch diameter. Average size just over two and one half inches diameter. The vessel was on its way to port after three days at sea in the offshore fishing grounds. The captain has fished the grounds for twenty-five years, reports this is the first time he has seen oil.

"Air Force aircraft patrolled the area within thirty minutes of the report and confirm the find. Samples taken from the water by helicopter and flown to Scripps Institution of Oceanography confirm the blobs comprise congealed crude oil of Prudhoe Bay consistency, biodegraded by micro-organisms and congealed by cold water. This oil is to be considered as the result of Mass Spill."

The voice paused. There was absolute silence in the room. Someone whispered, "Norwegian Sea!" The voice came back on.

"The vessel *Indian Reknown* reported at fifteen thirty-two hours she was now sailing in clear waters one hundred and seventeen nautical miles due south of Halifax. Air reconnaissance confirms no oil in her vicinity."

A scratching sound came from the speakers, and the green light flickered across the screen. The map faded and vanished, and a map of the eastern seaboard formed, from Cape Race to the Grand Banks.

"Commercial fishing has terminated on the Grand Banks. Maritime nations fishing the Banks have withdrawn all ships with the exception of three Russian factory ships that report they are processing their catches and standing by."

"The liner *Queen Elizabeth Two*, westbound one thousand, thirty-two nautical miles east of New York, has changed course from her Great Circle route to a course on latitude forty-three degrees. The vessel reports several slicks visible to the north, but is sailing in oil free waters, with the exception of occasional blobs.

The picture dissolved and was replaced by a chart of the sea between the Labrador Coast and the southern tip of Greenland.

"Oil is now observable from satellite intelligence across the width of Davis Strait. Slicks are from four to five miles wide. A concentration is flowing south in an offshore channel due to constriction in the Labrador Current. Flow measurements indicate a constant southerly flow of the oil mass at two and a quarter knots."

Admiral Culverton's head, silhouetted against the screen, snapped back.

"Water levels at Portugal Cove, Newfoundland, and Nova Scotia ports have stabilized but are above normal tide levels for this time of year. They are at record highs. Ponding off Portland, Maine, continues to build up, but emulsification has occurred in some localities and oil has been sighted in Massachusetts Bay off Boston, with traces of oil washed up at East Brewster and Barnstable Harbor on the north shore of Cape Cod——" A loud buzzing drowned out the flat voice.

"Lateflash! Lateflash! Report that oil has been sighted in Nantucket Sound is confirmed negative, repeat negative. End of Report: Mass Spill. Next report will be at eighteen hundred hours."

The screen went blank. Millwood blinked as the lights came on. An officer hurried across the floor and handed some papers to Culverton as a murmur of voices sounded from the head table. The Admiral thumped the table with his hand. "Order, please!"

The room quieted. Culverton sat erect, glancing down at the papers shaking in his hand.

"Here's more detailed data on what's happening in the north," he said, in a voice that hissed through the loudspeakers. "Oil concentration in the Labrador Current flowing west along the Nova Scotia coast is rapid. Computerized data on the depth of the oil on the surface, its specific gravity and constituency indicate a concentration of flow without dispersal."

The Admiral looked up. "This is the funnel through which oil feeds the ponding off Portland." He put down the papers and picked up a yellow teletype form.

"Here's the latest from the National Weather Service. 'Rapidly deteriorating weather off the Greenland coast indicates that you must consider decisive action in the next six hours.'"

Culverton got up. He crossed to the easel beside the big screen and loudly smacked the palm of his hand on the map of Davis Strait. "That," he said, "is where the solution to our problem lies. We must stop it here!"

"And burn off the pond at Portland!" Essenhigh shouted, rising.

"But the conveyor vessels are making headway with the flow." Meschino was on his feet, waving his pen in the air.

Essenhigh swung around. "Burn it! Get rid of it!" he said angrily.

Culverton sighed. In a tired voice he said, "Let's hear from our guest, Dr. Linzer." He nodded to a German scientist in the front row who had raised his hand. The man stood up as Culverton nodded at him.

"As I told our little group, our tests last August in the North Sea were most successful. With this new chemical compound we had an eighty-nine decimal three zero two percentage success rate. It ignites easier in cold water. The new——"

"On diesel oil, not crude!" Meschino cried shrilly.

Linzer regarded him coldly. "We have already stated that is so. But from theoretical extrapolations on flashpoints and molecular structures, we estimate it will ignite crude oil sixty-seven decimal zero four nine percentage of the times attempted."

Linzer reminded Millwood of a fellow captain who used figures to win arguments. "Choose an odd figure, like fifty-nine percent or sixty-one percent, never sixty percent," he'd said. "Nobody'll challenge it. Quote percentages to three decimal points, and everybody'll think you're a genius!"

"But your tests were in August," Meschino said, more calmly. "In relatively warm seas. The water temperature off Portland is less than sixty degrees this time of year in some places."

The German, a chemical expert from the Institute of Oceanography at Cuxhaven, stood his ground. Millwood marveled at the cool demeanor. It would take a rock to dislodge him now.

"Our figures prove quite conclusively that our method will succeed. Of that we are sure," he said, and sat down slowly, a thin dignified figure filled with stubborn self-confidence.

The Admiral gave a quick smile to a stubby man who had risen and who looked ill at ease in an obviously new suit. He ran a finger around the inside of his shirt collar and straightened his tie as he spoke.

"The new downward projecting air curtain we're developing in France has worked well on spills two kilometers in diameter, about a mile," he said rapidly. "We sucked up oil captured inside the circle of bubbles with conveyor belts mounted on ships." He turned from the Admiral and looked at Essenhigh. "We haven't had any experience with running tests on crude oil, monsieur, but we have had great success with Bunker C. And diesel oil—*pouff!*" He snapped his fingers in the air. "No problem!"

Culverton asked, "Do you recommend a burn-off, using your system?"

"Oh no, monsieur! It would damage the air curtain!"

"I thought so. What about the experiments with your device on crude, Prudhoe Bay type?"

"Ah, my colleague Monsieur Louis," the scientist said, turning to the man behind him. Louis was about thirty, with a red beard and rosy cheeks. He flipped open his briefcase and extracted a telegram.

"I have had a cable from our laboratory in Marseilles," he said in a deep voice. "They have done some preliminary work on the samples flown over." He raised his shoulders in a gesture of helplessness. "But it is too early! There has not been sufficient time! Perhaps we will hear soon!"

Culverton said, "Please tell me as soon as you hear. Your efforts are appreciated. Yes, Commodore?" He indicated a Coast Guard officer who had attracted his attention.

"Excuse my butting in, sir. Commodore Haynes. I flew in earlier from Davis Strait, from Captain Reed's vessel. I'm throwing out the suggestion we build a boom around the ponding oil off Portland, and then burn it off if the conveyor vessels can't lick it up fast enough."

"The trouble is, Commodore," Culverton said, fingering the pile of papers on the table, "a great many of the boom sections have been lost, washed ashore on Labrador or flotsam off Newfoundland. A few thousand have been retrieved by rescue ships, and a twenty-six-mile section has been towed to St. John's. Unfortunately, we used everything we had across Davis Strait. But we're ordering more in a hurry."

Culverton continued: "As chairman of this coordinating team, I say we give priority to stopping the southward drift of oil in Davis. We can deal with the ponding later, or with luck concurrently. But top priority goes to stopping the flow south. Do I have agreement? Let's have a show of hands."

Almost every hand was raised. Millwood had the impression most people had been waiting just for this: for the Admiral to make a firm suggestion. Essenhigh was in favor. He could see his pudgy hand sticking out from a buttonless shirt cuff.

"That's settled then," Culverton said, looking relieved. He looked at the satellite map on the easel. "One severe problem is ice, floes and bergs. Many floes are completely covered with oil. It's too widely distributed for burn-off." He lowered his voice and spoke to the Coast Guard officers near him at the head table. Heads nodded in agreement. He turned to the audience.

"We'll split into the small groups again. Your terms of reference: a method to completely stop the oil flowing south of latitude fifty-five. While you're doing that, our executive team will discuss the burn-off off Portland."

"Sit with us, Captain?"

Millwood looked around. It was Essenhigh. "Okay, but this stuff is over my head."

"We need every contribution," replied Essenhigh, "however unorthodox." His agitation had subsided and his eyes sparkled behind the steel-rimmed glasses as he turned to Meschino. "How *are* your bugs doing? Level with me!"

"Pretty lousy," Meschino said in a low voice. "I heard from the labs before this session. The viscosity of Prudhoe crude considerably reduces the biodegradability factor. I had hoped for better results."

"Too bad!" Essenhigh exclaimed. "What's the factor?"

"Something less than eighty percent of Bunker C."

Essenhigh made a helpless gesture. "That rules out bugs."

"Not entirely. We could use them on some of the emulsified patches."

"In the north?" said Essenhigh. "In arctic cold?" Meschino pulled his beard thoughtfully.

"Here's our German friend," Essenhigh said, welcoming Dr. Linzer. "Are you joining us again? By the way, have you met Captain Millwood? He was the—" Essenhigh broke off.

Millwood put out his hand and shook the tall man's hand. The professor bowed and said: "Pleased to meet you, Captain." Millwood saw the cool eyes and stern demeanor behind the quick smile. "And this is one of his colleagues, Dr. Mueller. Dr. Mueller is in charge of experimental work on effects of emulsification on the combustion of oil at low temperatures at Hamburg University and has come up with——"

"Director of Oil Degradation on the littoral, also," interjected Linzer reprovingly.

"So sorry, Doctor," Essenhigh said quickly.

Mueller smiled and Matheson said, "That's good, Doctor, we'll need you on coastal clean-up problems when we've got the flow licked."

Millwood saw the puzzlement that flashed across Mueller's face. So did Essenhigh. "He means once we've got the oil up north and off Portland cleared away, we're going to need help to clean up the coast."

Matheson said, "Tons of it are being washed ashore on the rocks on Casco Bay up in Maine. The Canadians are yelling their heads off about the mess on the Nova Scotia coast. What do you make of the water levels in Newfoundland? Let's sit down, for God's sake. Here, right over here. You with us, Captain?"

Millwood hesitated. He was conscious of Essenhigh and the others looking at him, waiting for his reply.

"If there's a spare seat," he said offhandedly.

"Here, next to me." Essenhigh patted a chair and turned to Linzer as they got settled. "I'm interested in your North Sea tests. I read your report. But have you had any luck with lower flashpoints?"

The German took a deep breath. "There is no need for lower flashpoints," he said haughtily. "The chemical we have developed has a success factor of eighty-nine decimal three zero two percentage. And that's in sea water with a temperature as low as ten degrees Centigrade—uh—fifty degrees Fahrenheit. We drop many canisters of the compound on the oil, thus raising the probability factor and the success rate." He turned to Mueller and made an impatient gesture. Meschino sucked the end of his pencil, showing studied indifference to the professor. Scientists, Millwood was discovering, were much like everyone else. Jealous when someone else came up with a better idea than their own, envious of others' successes. He imagined Meschino, the brilliant young research chemist, in his laboratories, instructing his assistants, building and enlarging his empire, spending long hours writing detailed reports, publishing papers in the journals of learned societies. Over all this activity hung the hope that the oil-eating bacteria would prove to be the answer to all oil spills at sea. He'd be acclaimed in the highest scientific circles as a savior, another Pasteur, another Salk. Meschino's future career as a research chemist depended largely on the outcome of his work in this field. He'd probably press for more research funds, more equipment, and more personnel.

Millwood switched his attention to Linzer. He was a man about sixty, clean-shaven, with pale cheeks and clear eyes, and wispy hair combed straight back. He exuded a coldness that Millwood suspected was more to do with his austere appearance than his nature. He imagined him before a class of students, a figure of rigid discipline commanding absolute attention. But he seemed the type of man who later, in the quiet of his study, would invite in a timid student and explain with infinite patience the solution to the student's problem.

"If we're going to talk about cleaning up Davis Strait, fix up a satellite overview like the big screen," Linzer said to Essenhigh.

"To cover just Davis Strait?"

"Of course." Linzer's eyebrows lifted. He gave the impression that anyone who asked that type of question was not very bright.

Essenhigh hesitated, glowering at the professor. It was clear he didn't like the other's overbearing manner. I'll speak to the Admiral," he said at last, jumping up and striding over to where Culverton stood talking with a group of Coast Guard officers. Essenhigh dived into the small knot of men, his rotund, slant-shouldered form dwarfed by the erect military figures. One by one the officers stood aside as Essenhigh commandeered the Admiral's attention. Millwood saw Culverton bend to hear Essenhigh. After a moment Culverton strode to the technician fussing with the control panel near the blank electronic map at the end of the room. He gesticulated and turned and spoke to Essenhigh, whose face lit up.

"He's arranging it," he said breathlessly as he sat down. "They can beam it through microwave to the big screen, via helicopters hovering over the Strait. That way we'll get a constant and closer picture instead of a satellite overpass every ninety minutes." He looked at Linzer. "It was a good idea, Doctor," he conceded.

"That's a clear picture," Culverton said.

"My God, look at the size of that berg!" Meschino exclaimed, pointing to the screen. "It must weigh millions of tons."

"We did studies of towing icebergs at Memorial University, in St. John's. Towed one once that weighed more than eight million tons."

Millwood turned to look at the owner of the soft voice from the back of the room. The speaker was a slight man with a bald head, and a round face slowly coloring with embarrassment as other heads turned. The man looked down, but Culverton spotted him.

"That's interesting. Dr. Tadman. I hadn't realized your experiments in Newfoundland dealt with towing bergs. And of that weight. Tell us more about them."

The man rose slowly. "Our work was in connection with

offshore drilling rigs. We had to evaluate what would happen if a large berg floated down on a rig. We studied the dynamics of floating mountains, if you like." He smiled, and Culverton smiled back encouragingly.

As Tadman warmed to his subject he became less self-conscious. "Bergs, as we all know, don't follow any fixed route over the surface of the sea. They wander capriciously at the whim of currents, wind, and wave. Our problem was: How do you protect oil rigs anchored on the Continental Shelf when one of these monsters looms out of the fog and bears down on you, all ten million tons of it?"

"What the hell *do* you do?" someone said. There was a long silence.

"Shut down all drilling operations, pull up your drill stem, retract the rig's feet from the ocean bed, and yank up your anchors, fast!"

"Move off site?" Essenhigh said.

"Yes. Get the hell out of there, if you've had warning enough. Otherwise. . . ." The speaker made a hopeless gesture and sat down quickly.

"Complete wipeout," Essenhigh said, looking from the Newfoundland professor to Culverton.

Heads turned back to the screen, now filled with a mosaic of big black floes floating lazily around the massive iceberg at center screen. Oil splashed around the black-rimmed base of the berg. The waves sucked and drove forward on the mountain of ice, sailing with its convoy of smaller bergs broken from the vast northern ice field.

Culverton's eyes sought out Tadman. "What was your object in towing the bergs?" he said.

"Well, obviously, sir. To see if we could tow them around the rigs before they collided." He blushed again.

Culverton's not afraid to ask obvious questions, Millwood

thought. He'd attended Navy war councils where somebody had assumed something and consequently botched a naval operation with loss of life. He'd seen it twice on those Korean coastal patrols. It was heartening to see someone like Culverton in action.

Culverton turned to the technician at the control panel. "Switch the picture to Cape Dyer," he said.

"That'll be about a hundred miles north, sir."

"Yes."

The screen dimmed, and brightened to show a flat gray background dotted with black irregular shapes. The technician swiveled around in his chair. "This is from the Cape Dyer camera copter, sir. She's at six thousand feet."

"Tell him to come down. Give us a real close-up."

"Yes, sir." The picture dissolved. The technician swiftly rotated a knob to refocus the screen. The gray background darkened until jagged lines covered the whole surface of the sea, like a jigsaw puzzle. "Two hundred feet, sir."

"What are those jagged lines?" asked a Navy captain in the front row.

"The edges of floes buried in the oil," answered Matheson.

"It's incredible," Essenhigh exclaimed, rising to see better.

"You see why we've got to clean up here first," the Admiral said in a flat voice.

The room fell silent. Everybody watched the screen intently as the camera on the distant helicopter panned the area: a black surface ruffled by a wave pattern, a wasteland of liquid mud on which floated millions of acres of oil-soaked floes, a semisolid morass—the bulk of *North Star*'s cargo. From the air it looked solid, as though one could step off a ship and walk across it.

Millwood stiffened as an idea began to take shape in his mind. How much had Tadman said the bergs they'd towed weighed? Eight million tons? The floes on screen wouldn't weigh that much. They could easily be towed—even lifted by helicopter and taken ashore. A surge of excitement rose. Supposing. . . . No, it was too crazy! They'd laugh at him. But what if it was possible to tow or lift the oil-covered floes ashore? Just suppose. That would get rid of a hell of a lot of oil. The stuff must be thickly coated on the floes. The frigid temperature would see to that. And the floes almost covered the whole sea. If you got rid of the floes and the oil that covered them, you'd clean off more than 80 percent of the oil. At least in Davis Strait, where the floes packed tightly against each other.

But what about farther out, toward Greenland? There'd be open oil-covered water there. If only there was a way to cover the open sea with floes, where they could soak up the oil, and then tow or lift the floes ashore. It would be like freezing the sea so that the oil would become semisolid. You could physically carry it away then. Millwood was shivering with excitement.

"To repeat an old statement. We're open for ideas," Culverton said wearily.

"Tow the floes ashore—oil and all, sir." Millwood didn't recognize the husky voice that spoke, but he was forced to believe it was his as faces turned toward him. "Or airlift them by chopper."

Encouraged that nobody spoke, he went on. "If there's a way of freezing the oil in open water, we could tow that away too. But I don't know how you'd do that. I'm not a scientist."

"Christ!" someone whispered. "That's a new idea."

"Freeze the sea! Impossible!" a man at the back said.

Millwood swung around. "I didn't say freeze the sea. I said: Freeze the oil that's on the sea!"

Essenhigh jumped to his feet. "Someone *did* freeze oil on

the sea in Frobisher. It was diesel oil, leaked from a supply ship. They sprayed liquid nitrogen on it and the oil froze like a pancake! Grab me a phone, someone. I'll get the report on it!"

THIRTEEN

Millwood leaned against the bridge console as the destroyer sped through ice-covered seas, feeling the vibration when the specially reinforced bow hit the floes. Sailors pushed metal canisters into depth charge ejectors on the foredeck below him. Essenhigh, like a bear in a fleece-lined parka several sizes too large for him, ordered the men about. Millwood smiled. The sailors were taking it in good spirit; they had the air of men working with deliberate purpose. The lieutenant in charge stood aside as Essenhigh waved his arms and yelled for them to handle the frozen liquid carefully.

"Meschino's hit on a good idea with those canisters," Culverton said, watching the action. "Better than spraying. More controllable."

"If it works, we can drop them by helicopter."

"Bomb the oil with liquid nitrogen! That'll be something new, Captain."

Millwood crossed to the television monitor above the chart table. "There's a picture coming through, sir," he said. "That must be us. Sailing through a sea of oil!"

Culverton turned to the commander, at the helmsman's elbow. "This is a good place to start."

"Aye, aye, sir." Commander Calder, who looked less than thirty, and who probably never had had an admiral on his ship before, sprang to the telephone. Bells jangled noisily, and the destroyer glided to slow speed.

Culverton turned to Calder. "If your depth charge launchers are loaded, Commander, prepare to fire the canisters downwind, to port."

"Aye, aye, sir." He spoke again into the telephone and looked out of the window. Essenhigh nodded. The lieutenant raised his hand to signify everything was ready.

Culverton looked at the sky, drawing Millwood's eyes upward. Four helicopters hovered overhead.

"Lifting helicopters on station." He turned to the Commander. "Fire canisters!"

Calder bent forward and spoke into the telephone. Millwood stared at the oily sea through which the vessel slipped at slow speed. Two cracks resounded: two dark shapes flew in high arcs from the ship. They fell into the sea about fifty yards away, hardly splashing as the oil cushioned their fall. Culverton grabbed a pair of binoculars. Millwood stared at the place where the canisters had dropped through the oil surface. A boiling motion disturbed the surface of the sea. Froth appeared. Then the waves rippled over the spot and the canisters vanished.

Culverton groaned. "Fire the next two, Commander!"

More canisters rose from the deck and hit the sea. The result was a boiling action, froth and nothing more.

"The damned things sink before the liquid nitrogen has a chance to spread!" Essenhigh shouted. He had left the foredeck and joined the others on the bridge.

"Spraying from the deck might be better," Culverton suggested.

Essenhigh shook his head. "Too dangerous. If the wind swings around the ship'll be sprayed." He thumped his fist against the edge of the console. "There's got to be a way! There's got to be!"

Millwood turned to the Admiral. "You mentioned bombing, sir," he said. "What about tying a parachute to the canisters so they'll come down softly on the oil and give the stuff time to spread?"

Culverton was silent, frowning at the spot where oil surged above the disappearing canisters. "It's worth trying. What about it, Doctor?" he asked wearily.

"Anything's worth a try now," Essenhigh replied in a resigned voice.

The radio telephone gave two sharp rings. "I'll take it," Culverton said.

"No—no success yet. We're trying something new. What's going on down there?" The radio officer pressed a button, and Meschino's voice filled the bridge.

"The burn-off's a fifty-fifty success. The oil to the north, where it's slipping down the Labrador Current, is burning off okay. But the emulsified stuff on the southern front won't burn at all—too much water. Our German friend says it needs more of his chemical compound, Kontax. He guarantees it'll reach flashpoint then."

There was a pause, as if Meschino was looking over his shoulder to see if Linzer was within earshot. He continued in a low voice. "Frankly, sir, I don't think it'll work. Too much water in the oil and it's dispersing fast."

"Toward Boston?" The Admiral's voice tightened.

"Yes, sir. But the boom's up around the harbor entrance."

"I know," Culverton said impatiently. "How fast is the emulsified oil flowing south?"

"Half an hour ago it was doing a steady four knots. There's a moderate northeast wind helping it along. The latest meteorological report calls for a veering strengthening wind."

Culverton groaned. "That'll swing it into the coast. Have you warned the Coast Guard?"

"Yes, Admiral." Meschino's voice sounded tired. The cheerful tone Millwood remembered from the early conferences had gone. Meschino and the others had been on continual duty for six days, with only catnaps. Millwood realized how tired his own body was. He stroked his cheek. The quick shave he'd had in the crowded officers' wardroom had left a stubble. He glanced out of the bridge window at the sea, covered with an opaque sheen as the sunlight caught the ebony slant of the waves. The ship had come almost to a standstill, nudging into the light swell from the northeast. The oily waters stretched away, changing from black to iron gray in the middle distance and fading to a hardened ashen brown where the sky met the horizon. He looked across the foredeck. The depth charge crew stood at ease, waiting expectantly for instructions. A squadron of eight helicopters hovered overhead.

"How long do you think it'll take to burn up the oil in the northern sector?"

"Several hours, sir. Eight or ten," Meschino replied doubtfully. How ironical it was, Millwood thought, that young, ambitious Meschino, the man who had hoped to develop an oil-eating strain of bacterium, should be put in charge of the burn-off, which at one point he had opposed. But then, there had been many ironies and paradoxes since he'd set sail in *North Star*.

"What do you base that on?" Culverton cut in irritably.

"The time it took to burn off what we've already burned, sir. With this freshening breeze, it might burn faster."

"Keep me informed. What's happening to the smoke?"

"There's a trail several miles long lifting at the coast. We've had complaints."

"Who from?"

"City officials in Portland and towns farther inland. They're threatening to sue the Coast Guard, the Navy and company—the lot."

"Tell 'em to go ahead!" Culverton thundered, and slammed down the telephone.

"Stupid bastards!" he muttered. He turned to Essenhigh. "Are we ready, Doctor?" he said in a calmer voice.

"All set, sir."

The Admiral turned to the Commander. "Keep as little way on as possible. I want this test to be made while we're almost stopped. Give the liquid nitrogen a chance to spread over the oil. Got it?"

"Minimum way it is, sir."

"Depth charge crew ready?" Culverton said.

Calder grabbed a phone. "Prepare to fire!" he said. He turned to Culverton. "Ready, sir."

"On your time."

Millwood saw the Commander's lips move silently. He stared over Essenhigh's shoulder at the foredeck. Two canisters flew high into the air and hung like twin satellites poised between sky and sea. Two red parachutes broke out, fluttered indecisively, and ballooned into mushroom shapes. The canisters jerked abruptly, steadied, and started to descend, swinging from side to side as the wind caught them. A hundred feet, ninety, eighty—they moved so slowly that Millwood wondered if Essenhigh had miscalculated the size of the parachutes. Firmly in the wind's grip now, they crossed the ship's bow and moved off to port. Seventy-five feet, sixty, fifty feet up, a hundred yards off the side of the ship. Forty, thirty, twenty feet from the surface. Culverton grabbed the binoculars. Millwood stepped with the others to the side of the bridge. The canisters fell in a trough and vanished.

"God, another failure!" He was about to turn away when the canisters reappeared, bobbing on a wave crest. They jerked spasmodically as the canister valves opened. Two puffs of white vapor appeared and a filmy gray mist began to spread over the oil.

"It's working!" Essenhigh yelled. "The nitrogen's spreading!"

"By God! I think we've done it!" Culverton shouted. "Bring her to a full stop, Commander."

"Aye, aye, sir."

"It's spreading fast now!" Essenhigh cried. "It's covered fifty yards!"

The Admiral took the binoculars from his eyes. "The question is, what'll it do to the oil?"

"Give it a chance! It worked in the test tank!"

Millwood watched the carpet of mist creep over the sea, giving it the patina of mildew. A convoy of ice floes bore down on the canisters, pushing them close to the vessel.

"Look!" Essenhigh exclaimed. "It's freezing the oil on the floes!"

"You're right," Millwood said slowly. He was almost afraid to believe that the nightmare might be beginning to end. He peered at the floes as they drifted alongside. The black scum was solidified, like frozen molasses on a white plate. Even the oily water between the floes appeared solid.

"It's congealing the oil on the water too," he said. "Look, sir!" He pointed at the sea.

Culverton's leathery face lit up. "Essenhigh, you landlubber of a seadog, you've done it!"

"It was a real seadog who planted the idea in my head," Essenhigh said, clapping his hand around Millwood's neck.

"Commander," Culverton said, regaining his composure, "get the helicopters to try the lifting apparatus."

"Aye, aye, sir."

Millwood glanced up. The lead helicopter advanced. Hanging vertically beneath it was a gridded frame. The pilot maneuvered the helicopter skillfully until the frame was suspended three feet above the congealed layer of oil on the surface. The frame suddenly splashed vertically into the sea and vanished. A large rectangular shape emerged from the sea, streaming water. The frame had been turned horizontal under the surface by the slip-ring and guy ropes, and was now hoisting a weight of oil and muck from the sea. The sparkle of clear water appeared below it.

"Call in the others, Admiral!" Essenhigh shouted.

Culverton nodded to Calder. The second helicopter moved into position, its frame skimming the surface. Another huge rectangle of frozen oil rose from the sea.

Culverton shook his head. "It'll take years to clean it up this way. Think of the square miles of sea we have to cover. We need surface vessels, like those log-boom tugs down in Newfie."

"What are they?" Essenhigh asked.

"Ocean-going tugs that tow big rafts of pulpwood logs up and down the coast of Newfoundland. They use them on the West Coast too," Millwood explained. He turned to Culverton. "A circular log boom to collect the congealed oil and tow it ashore. Is that it, sir?"

"Yes. Some of those tugs can handle a raft a mile long.

They can easily tow an elongated pool of oil five miles long at slow speed."

"We'll need a combination of methods," Essenhigh interjected. "Helicopters lifting oil congealed by liquid nitrogen for the tricky inshore areas and the boom tugs, hundreds of them, across the open water in Davis Strait and elsewhere. The inshore oil should stay semisolid long enough to handle after we've frozen it with the nitrogen. If it shows signs of unfreezing we'll drop more nitrogen on it—even though it's expensive stuff." He pointed to the third helicopter clearing a path through the floes.

Culverton watched the helicopter for a moment in silence. "It won't be as easy as that," he said soberly. "There'll be oil in these waters and in the Atlantic for years to come, where it's been pooling in the confluences of ocean currents. And the rocks and sands off the eastern seaboard will show traces of oil even after we clean up, right down to Cape Cod. There's simply no way to wash oil away completely."

He nodded toward the starboard side of the bridge. "Not to mention the damage up north. Up in Kivitooluk and those other Eskimo villages. Matheson reports there's been irreversible damage done to the Arctic ecology in localized areas. Christ, this should be warning enough for the oil industry—and for the whole world."

FOURTEEN

The television cameras had eagerly fastened on Millwood when he had been called to testify. Thinking about it now, sitting in the Senate conference room for the fifth day, he was surprised how quickly he had become used to the camera's stare under the hot floodlights, concentrating on his retelling of the account of *North Star*'s voyage, from the moment he'd instructed Harding to cast off from Prudhoe terminal to the instant he'd ordered the lowering of the raft down the side and the abandonment of *North Star*. The inquiry chairman, Senator Burtram W. Vidaver, head of the United States delegation to the Inter-governmental Maritime Consultative Organization, politely thanked him and complimented him on presenting a concise account. When the chairman invited questions, only one man, a crusty old senator from California who represented Alaskan oil pipeline interests, asked a question.

"What is your considered opinion, Captain Millwood, of the feasibility of operating completely crewless, that is, fully automated, submarine oil tankers under the Northwest Passage as had been proposed by the company that employs you?"

"On paper, feasible. In practice, not feasible," he replied emphatically. He'd sure as hell never advocate running even manned submarine tankers under the ice again.

Tall, powerfully built, the chairman looked and acted every inch the leader of an official government inquiry. Millwood hoped he would wrap it up today. The conference room, he'd discovered by adroitly questioning the aged retainer who guarded the door, had been reserved for only five days. The chairman's voice penetrated his consciousness:

". . . and find myself in the position of both judge and advocate. The evidence has been ably presented by the representatives of the submarine's constructors, Captain Millwood as official observer at the scientific coordination center, his crew members, the Coast Guard, Navy, members of the scientific coordinating task force, the officials of Prudhoe-Northwest Passage Corporation, and by officers from Cape Dyer and elsewhere. The facts as presented are clear. We agree on those." He glanced to the left and right, taking in the other members of the inquiry.

The paneled door behind the chairman opened noiselessly. A secretary entered, silently crossed to the chairman, put a file folder down in front of him, and retired. The chairman fingered the file absent-mindedly before opening it.

"We've read the brief presented by Admiral Culverton, Chairman of the President's Panel on Oil Spills. His work in organizing the Scientific Coordination Task Force has been praised during the course of this inquiry. We have decided to make public this brief. It contains excellent recommendations, some of which were contained in the original report of the President's Panel, but were ignored. In light of current history, we cannot ignore certain facts about the grave danger to the ocean environment of the world. It is no exaggeration to say that the oceans of the globe are dangerously close to extinction. Some experts give it ten, others twenty, some fifty years, before it will be finished as a living dynamic organism. And life on land depends on a living ocean environment."

He paused, looked down at the file folder briefly, and went on.

"Some of these facts I am about to repeat are well known, but I want them read into the record. More than seventy per cent of the earth's surface is covered by the oceans. Sixty per cent of the earth's surface is international waters. In these international waters there are no laws that prevent anybody from polluting. You may this afternoon take a little rowing boat, go outside the territorial limits of the United States, and throw overboard a drumful of oil or any garbage you like. Nobody's going to stop you, nobody's going to arrest you. There are no policemen on the high seas." He paused dramatically to allow his words to sink in. "In the natural decomposition of oil in sea water, one gallon of oil depletes the oxygen in four hundred thousand gallons of water.

"Also for the record, oil pollution is not the only ecological problem we have in mind. There is no international agreement to curtail whaling. Whales are now in danger of extinction. There is criminal overexploitation of pelagic fishing grounds. There is a lesson to be learned on what has just happened on the Grand Banks. Nuclear bombs continue to be tested in what were remote islands, and their fallout contaminates the oceans. Lethal chemicals are dumped into the oceans by the thousands of tons every year by several governments, including our own. If individual people and government officials acted this way on the land surface they would be imprisoned. Why do we allow this destruction of the seas to go on?

RAGE UNDER THE ARCTIC

"Samples of plankton from the Atlantic have been found to contain an unsuspected amount of industrial pollutants called polychlorinated biphenyls, something like the DDT every living creature on earth now has in its body tissue. Fish eat plankton and men eat fish. I don't have to tell this audience what this means.

"We see how oil companies fight and lobby for the right to exploit oil resources lying under the continental shelves of many parts of the world. In the ocean deeps lie other natural resources that greedy entrepreneurs eye. There are an estimated several billion dollars' worth of manganese nodules on the ocean bed, containing not only manganese but valuable amounts of cobalt, copper, and nickel. Private industry is gearing up to harvest them. We'll see anarchy on the high seas unless an international law of the seas is framed, with an international police force to enforce the law.

"President Lyndon Johnson once said, and I quote: 'We must ensure that the deep sea and the ocean bottom are and remain the legacy of all human beings.' "

He shoved the papers to one side. "What legacy are we leaving behind? International law or piracy? It took many years after air and water pollution became serious in the United States and elsewhere for the United Nations to hold a Conference on the Human Environment in Stockholm. The United Nations recently held a Law of the Seas Conference. The Human Environment Conference produced a long-winded preamble and twenty-six principles of the common rights of all the peoples of the world. Everybody clapped and adopted them. The Law of the Seas Conference came out with similar principles and recommendations. High-sounding phrases and good intentions are easily mouthed. The real test is to apply these principles, to embody them in international law, to enforce them—and to make them work."

Culverton and the members of his task force leaned forward. The military officers in the front row were motionless. The television camera operators were intent as they focused on the chairman.

"The United Nations lacks both legal and financial means to implement laws. Its terminology is shallow. The word *law* becomes *recommendation*, which means nothing. The UN is broke. Nations ignore appeals to pay dues. We say there must be no delay in applying the Ocean Development Tax worked out by economists at Cambridge University. I have the details here for anybody who wants to see them later." He held up a sheaf of papers.

"What these boil down to is simple. If you exploit the world's oceans you pay a royalty, yes, even for fishing. So much a ton of fish landed, so much a ton of manganese nodules dredged up, so much a ton for whales killed, so much a ton for *any* resource from the sea. Like the royalty payments oil companies now make for every barrel they pump up from under the sea."

He wiped the perspiration from his forehead and looked hard at the televsion lens beneath the floodlights.

"The money raised—it will run into billions of dollars over a few years but raise the cost of commercial fishing only a tiny fraction—will be used to finance a police force of fast patrol ships and aircraft, train technicians, do research on ocean pollution and conservation, and provide an antipollution force to prevent, contain and, if necessary, clean up accidental oil pollution such as the catastrophe we are now dealing with.

"Which brings me to the bare bones of Admiral Culverton's brief. The first of these urges that the United States Government immediately unifiy its own pollution agencies and take over state authorities to form a single, strongly organized, central antipollution force of ships, conveyor ships, boom control vessels, scientists, technicians, and paramilitary force that can be rushed to the scene of an oil spill."

Vidaver took a deep breath and continued in a strong voice.

"The legal side of oil spills must be thrashed out. At the moment international law, if we can call it that, doesn't allow any ship to go to the rescue of a damaged tanker without the permission of the stricken ship's captain, if the ship is in international waters. We've got to fix blame and liability. As things now stand nobody can be blamed and punished. Oil companies owning a tanker quickly pay out to clean up coastal regions polluted by oil. They do it because it's good public relations, not from any heartfelt need to protect the environment. They must be induced to make foolproof tankers and make sure all safety regulations have been carried out——"

A thickset man leaped to his feet, his face distorted in anger. "That's not fair!" he cried.

"The time to present briefs and make verbal comments ended at twelve noon today," the chairman said sternly.

The man persisted. "I just flew in from——"

"Then you've missed your chance to be heard. I cannot——"

"The tanker industry won't put up with such calumny, distortions of fact, and downright lies!" the man yelled.

"This hearing is public and so far has been conducted in an orderly manner. If you continue to interrupt, I shall have you ejected," declared the chairman.

"Tanker owners take *all precautions* on safety. Put that in your record!"

The chairman nodded to the guard, who left his position at the rear door and moved closer to the angry man. When he was about six feet away the man sat down, and the chairman continued.

"The brief recommends, and we endorse the recommendation, new regulations to be written into the specifications for all new tankers designed after next January first. The Society of Naval Architects and Marine Engineers will be asked to draw up mandatory specifications for tankers. We recommend inspection of tankers before they leave port—including the navigation systems and equipment—and the on-loading port facilities, plus inspection during off-loading at the port of destination. Oil tankers are in traffic jams in harbors and ports, maneuvering into oil-discharging terminals with only inches to spare. The chances of even more serious accidents occurring increases daily. Nearly seventy-five per cent of accidents at sea are attributable to human error. Seventy per cent take place within three nautical miles of shore. Tankers are getting bigger. Half-a-million-tonners are now at sea, slipping into tight port facilities, and one-million-tonners are on the drawing boards. Already one large tanker has exploded near a port, at Kawasaki, Japan. Two large tankers collided off South Africa recently. When and where will the next accident occur?" The chairman picked up a piece of paper. He pulled out eyeglasses from his breast pocket and adjusted them on his nose.

"Here are the latest figures from *Lloyd's Register of Shipping*. Every day, one of the sixty thousand ocean-going commercial ships of the world sinks. Forty thousand oil tankers are at sea. They haul eleven billion barrels of oil a year. Oil consumption is doubling every ten years due to the energy shortage, principally in the United States. Ship traffic is at an all-time high; so are sinkings. Three hundred and fifty-two ships in 1970, up forty per cent over the six previous years. Million-ton tankers would take ten sea miles to stop. Imagine such a monster laden with crude colliding dockside in New Jersey!"

A cry of protest came from the back of the room. "Who's going to pay? Tanker, oil, and port terminal costs will shoot sky high!"

"Insurance rates will go down!" a man at the front shouted back.

"Order! I must have order!" the chairman demanded. "Officer!" He motioned to the guard who hesitated, undecided in which direction to move as other voices broke into a hubbub, then gradually died away.

The chairman said, "Marine insurance rates have jumped forty percent in the past three years. Oil companies pay more than one million dollars a year in premiums on supertankers weighing over two hundred and fifty thousand tons. This rate is bound to drop if tanker operations were made safer as a result of our recommendations. Of course some of the ideas proposed by this board of inquiry are going to cost money to implement. We believe the burden should fall on those who profit most from the exploitation of natural resources. Safer tankers may cost more to build. Safer port facilities will cost more. Inspection services are going to cost money."

A lanky man jumped up and cupped his hands to his lips to project his voice. "And oil's going to cost more!" He sat down quickly.

"You can say that again!" This time the outburst was from the chairman's left. "I represent the Petroleum Association of——"

"Sit down, please!" The chairman's voice was firm.

"I will not sit down while this committee of inquiry spouts rules that will cost the public money for a commodity that the petroleum producers of the United States are now providing at the least possible——"

"Sit down or be thrown out!" the chairman commanded angrily, slapping the table with the palm of his hand. The man stood his ground defiantly, looking from side to side, seeking support from the audience. The floodlights turned on him. The chairman hesitated. "Plenty of time has been allowed all interested parties at this inquiry to state their views," he said in an effort to get the lights and cameras back to him. The cameramen, sensing hot news shots, kept their cameras pointing at the oilman, who, feeling victory, announced in a loud clear voice: "Oil producers will fight legislation proposed under the pretense of antipollution measures——"

"*I* won't fight it!"

Millwood swung around as a familiar voice bellowed from the back of the room. It was Simoncelli. "I'll go along with proposals for better safety regulations to transport oil, on the high seas or anywhere else!" he said loudly, taking a step down the aisle.

"Order!" This time the chairman's voice was tempered with restraint.

"I control forty-two percent of southern oil producers and thirty-odd percent of this country's tanker fleets, and I'll personally guarantee to implement new rules to prevent oil pollution at sea." He smiled at the chairman and beamed at the audience.

The bald man from the Petroleum Association slowly sat down. The television cameras swiveled to focus on Simoncelli as he marched noisily down the aisle and lowered his broad bottom into a vacant seat. An inquiry-board member near the chairman scribbled something on a notepad and passed it to the chairman, who looked at it and nodded.

"My colleague reminds me that I have three other points to make on tanker safety regulations we will urge the government to adopt in conjunction with the maritime nations working through the UN. One is that special sea lanes be set aside across the oceans for the use of tankers only. The second is that research be intensified immediately to devise a worldwide automatic electronic navigation system for tankers to check the manual navigation systems now used. This electronic system should be done via satellite and nuclear-powered buoys. The third is that monitoring stations be set up around the world—including the Arctic regions—to detect oil pollution automatically."

"Damned good idea," someone murmured.

"I have here a list of some of the lawsuits filed by various parties claiming damages as a result of the *North Star* catastrophe," the chairman went on solemnly. "I'm sure there are plenty more to come in. Commonwealth of Massachusetts, City of Boston, State of Maine, Provinces of Newfoundland and Nova Scotia; the British Colonial Office gives notice it is holding the United States Government to blame for oil pollution on the coast of Bermuda, and here's a bill from the Cunard company for cleaning the hull of the liner *Queen Elizabeth Two*. It runs into several hundred thousand pounds. Other writs, by the State of Maine and certain commercial fishing interests, for example, run into several millions of dollars. Damages are also claimed by the governments of the Soviet Union, Japan, Canada, Spain, Portugal, Norway, Denmark, Britain, West and East Germany, and other sovereign states for damages resulting to ships, equipment, and loss of commercial fish catches on the Grand Banks fishing grounds. Most suits are against the Prudhoe-Northwest Passage Corporation—but some are against the United States government."

He fumbled for a slip of paper that had stuck between some larger sheets, and looked up with a half smile. "And here's a claim from the captain of a vessel based on the Faeroes, for twenty-two dollars and forty-one cents for cleaning the hull of a fishing boat named *Thorhalla*. The bill is broken down into the cost of five and a half gallons of cleaning fluid plus labor charges based on those current in the island." A ripple of laughter sounded near the front row.

"If I'd been the chairman I'd have thrown you out!" Millwood said.

Simoncelli purred with leonine contentment. "Why me, Frank?" he retorted. "I was the only guy who agreed with him!"

"*Shhh!* There he goes now. Just getting into his car."

The inquiry had just concluded. The sun shone from a clear sky, outlining the white obelisk of the Washington Monument in the distance. The steps were crowded with people drifting from the Senate committee room, talking in little groups or making their way toward the sidewalk. A tall figure suddenly detached itself from a group at the doorway and strode toward him. It was Culverton.

"Congratulations, Captain!" he said, shaking Millwood's hand warmly. "I never doubted that they'd exonerate you."

"Thank you, Admiral."

"How's it going, Admiral?" Simoncelli said.

"Boston Harbor's open and the fishing fleet's put out for the Grand Banks. They've got most of the fishing grounds skimmed off. And the big ponding off Portland's about seventy-five percent cleared. But the coastal clean-up—" He made a helpless gesture. "The entire Maine coast and a large part of the Massachusetts coast is covered in oil. The rocks on Casco Bay, where the tankers pass on their way into Portland refineries, are thick with it well above low-water mark. Matheson reports it's worse there than at Kivitooluk. The ecology of the East Coast and up north will be adversely affected for years: fishing, bird life, everything." He looked at his watch. "I've got a meeting with Matheson and his crew. Good luck, Captain." He gripped Millwood's hand firmly.

"Good luck to you, sir. And thank you."

Culverton shook Simoncelli's hand. Simoncelli said earnestly, "If you want support for the new legislation, you can get me in Houston."

Culverton hurried away. "I'm off to the airport, Frank," Simoncelli said. "My pilot's picking me up in half an hour. I'll see you around the company next week. By the way, Herbert Armstrong told me he's thinking of going ahead with *North Star*'s proposed sister subs but converting them into transatlantic cargo carriers. He'll be looking for skippers. So long!"

"Hey!" Millwood said, but Simoncelli was already lumbering down the steps with his unbuttoned jacket flapping in the breeze. A Lincoln Continental swiftly rolled up to the curb, a chauffeur got out and held the rear door open, and the old man clambered in.

Millwood looked around. The crowd had melted away. A few stragglers talked in little groups, lawyers carrying official-looking attaché cases. A feeling of loneliness swept over him. The worries and crises of the past three weeks had dissipated, leaving an empty feeling. He checked his watch. Six-thirty. His plane for Boston didn't leave until tomorrow morning. The prospect of an evening and night alone in Washington spread before him. He hated the idea of going back to his hotel and eating there. Maybe he'd run into someone he knew at the Naval Officers' Club, have dinner there, and then stroll along the Potomac and see what ships were moored in the Navy Yard. He turned on his heel and walked down the steps.

"Frank!"

He swung around. Eva was running down the steps, her white teeth gleaming in an eager smile, sandy hair flying. In a moment she was in front of him. "I missed you on the way out," she exclaimed breathlessly. "Lost a shoe in the crowd—broken strap. I had to go back to find it. Look!" She held up the broken shoe triumphantly.

"Let's see if we can do some running repairs!" Millwood laughed, his spirits suddenly soaring. "Tie this strap this way, like so. A reef knot here, and *presto!* Simple!"

" 'Electronics engineers only know about complicated things'," she quoted with a mischievous giggle. Her smile faded as she gazed at him earnestly. "I'm so glad about the way the inquiry turned out for you, Frank. We all knew you'd be exonerated, of course, and I was so proud of you on the stand! You were wonderful. I . . ."

She bent quickly to hide her crimson face, and thrust her foot into the mended shoe. "There, good as new," she declared, stamping to test the strap. She took his hand to steady herself, and Millwood held it firmly when she tried to draw it away.

"Eva, we've got some things to celebrate," he announced. "Beginning with dinner for two in a nice quiet spot. I know just the place, not far from the Naval Officers' Club . . . but far enough." He guided her down the steps and waved.

"Taxi!"